"I told you perfectly happy to raise this child alone..." she reminded him, striving to keep her voice steady even as she felt as if she was suddenly hovering over a minefield and, with any step, there would be an explosion.

"And I'm telling you today that whatever you thought yesterday is not acceptable to me." His eyes glowed down at her in a way that made her far too aware of the unfettered leaping of her heart and pulse. "There is no world in which any child of mine will grow up without my name, or without me being in their life. So, you and I are going to get married."

The word detonated in Serena's ears, disorienting both her body and mind, and it was a moment before the daze cleared enough for her to form words. "Married?" she repeated, hoping he would tell her that she had misheard him, but that hope sank as he made a single, controlled gesture of his dark head. She shook her head, backing away from him and from the treacherous frissons that were firing through her at the thought.

Rosie Maxwell has dreamed of being a writer since she was a little girl. Never happier than when she is lost in her own imagination, she is delighted that she finally has a legitimate reason to spend hours every day dreaming about handsome heroes and glamorous locations. In her spare time, she loves reading—everything from fiction to history to fashion—and doing yoga. She currently lives in the North West of England.

Also by Rosie Maxwell

Harlequin Presents

An Heir for the Vengeful Billionaire
Billionaire's Runaway Wife

Visit the Author Profile page at Harlequin.com.

PREGNANT AND CONVENIENTLY WED

ROSIE MAXWELL

PRESENTS

MIX
Paper | Supporting responsible forestry
FSC® C021394
www.fsc.org

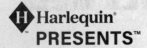

Harlequin®
PRESENTS™

Recycling programs for this product may not exist in your area.

ISBN-13: 978-1-335-21345-7

Pregnant and Conveniently Wed

Harlequin Enterprises ULC
22 Adelaide St. West, 41st Floor
Toronto, Ontario M5H 4E3, Canada
www.Harlequin.com

HarperCollins Publishers
Macken House, 39/40 Mayor Street Upper,
Dublin 1, D01 C9W8, Ireland
www.HarperCollins.com

Printed in Lithuania

PREGNANT AND CONVENIENTLY WED

CHAPTER ONE

THIS WAS THE part of the evening that Serena Addison loathed the most. The part when her friends went off in one direction and she had to go another.

Tonight, it was worse than usual because she wasn't just missing out on after-work drinks at the pub around the corner from where they worked in London, she was missing out on a once-in-a-lifetime experience in Singapore. Missing out on a nightclub that was not only the hottest club in the city, but one of the most talked about nightlife venues in the world right now. And she knew the soundtrack to tomorrow morning would be her friends excited chatter as they relived their exploits in annoyingly exhaustive detail, and she would have to listen and smile with interest, all the while pretending she wasn't seething that she was missing out yet again, hearing about their experiences instead of living her own. And that was so goddamned maddening, Serena wanted to scream with the force of her frustration.

'You could come with us, you know,' Evie, her closest friend, had whispered to her earlier. 'We're seven thousand miles away from London and from evil Marcia. She'll never know what you do tonight.'

It was tempting to believe that, but living in a world dominated by social media rendered those seven thousand miles meaningless, and Serena knew it. She had said as much to Evie too. It would take only one photograph of her drinking and dancing with her friends for her stepmother to follow through with the heinous threats she loved to issue and banish Serena from the family home and, even more devastatingly, sever her contact with her younger brother and sister, which as their adoptive mother she had every right to do. But that was not a price Serena was willing to pay.

Being separated from Kit and Alexis wasn't an option. It never had been. Having helped to take care of them from the first day of their lives after the heartbreaking loss of their mother during childbirth, their bond was far beyond that of normal siblings, and after the unexpected and upending death of their father almost six years ago, she was the only blood family they had. And they were hers, so it was imperative they stay together.

Not just because Serena grew heartsick at the thought of breaking the promise she had made to her mother during her pregnancy—that she would always be there for her younger siblings—but because she'd already endured all the loss she could stomach.

Her mum, then her dad and then the baby she'd been carrying when she was eighteen years old. She'd only been ten weeks pregnant and the situation had been far from ideal, especially after the boyfriend she'd thought she could count on had fled, but Serena had formed such a strong attachment to her pregnancy that the loss of it had been a body blow, and without loving parents there to support her, it had been the hardest loss by far. It was in that moment that she'd known she didn't want to endure any more of that pain and had vowed to never again put herself in the position where she would lose someone else.

But even knowing that didn't stop a hotter than usual frustration burning through her blood as she watched Evie and the other girls disappear into the glowing darkness of the nightclub. Didn't stop her heart from pounding with heavy, sickly thuds because she wanted so badly to be with them. To sip colourful cocktails and dance the night away. More than anything she wanted to have some fun and not spend another evening alone, excruciatingly aware of everything she was missing out on. But that was not an option. Not as long as she had her stepmother's beady eyes scrutinising her every move, she thought with a thick surge of resentment.

There had never been any closeness between them. In all the years of being in her life, her stepmother had never shown Serena a shred of love or support or understanding. Not even when her father had died, and definitely not even when she'd suffered her miscarriage. Bewildered as to what had happened and why, Serena had been desperate for a set of comforting arms to hold her and would have welcomed that even from her cold stepmother, but all she had offered was the unfeeling sentiment of *it's probably for the best,* as though Serena would have made a hopeless mother. She'd had to find the strength within herself to pick up the pieces and pull herself up, and she had, only for Marcia to strike again. Untrusting of Serena to not bring scandal and shame to their name again, she had stymied her plans, *dreams*, of attending art school. Serena knew she hadn't been an angel, especially not after her father had passed away and she'd sought escape from her grief in letting loose with her friends, but the punishment hardly seemed fair. Unless she'd wanted to lose Kit and Alexis, Serena's only choice was to endure it.

And endure it she had, along with all of Marcia's other ridiculous and oppressive rules, for five long years.

No revealing clothes. No late nights. No bars or nightclubs. No freedom. No fun. The list went on and on and on…

Although it had been worth it to remain close to Kit and Alexis, the sacrifices had never been easy, and lately Serena felt more exasperated than ever before with all the limitations, frustration bubbling away deep inside and pushing ever closer to the surface. More and more often she caught herself longing for the day when she would finally escape her stepmother's clutches and be free to live as she wanted.

Soon, Serena reminded herself on a steadying breath, because she could feel the aggravation building afresh. The twins would turn twelve on their next birthday, and with another year or two, when they had more autonomy over their lives and Marcia couldn't prevent them from seeing her, then she could seize and embrace her freedom. But until then, she had to play by Marcia's rules. If she wanted to remain in Kit's and Alexis's lives, she had no other choice. And she'd survived all this time. She could put up with it for another few years. At least that was what she kept telling herself.

It wasn't as if it was all bad. Living within Marcia's tight boundaries had prevented her from getting close to anyone, from searching for love in the wrong place as she had done with Lucas. She had not been able to expose herself to any more of the heartbreak and loss that had been delivered to her in two cruel blows—his desertion and then her miscarriage. For that, at least, she was grateful.

But they've stopped you from experiencing anything else either.

That thought sounded so loudly in her head that it inflamed every bad feeling she already had. Aware that she needed to act to keep her mood from plummeting any lower, Serena spun on her heel and started to walk purposefully towards the elevators, knowing exactly what she would do. If she was at home, she would lock herself away in her little attic annex and vent her frustration through creation, spewing her feelings across her canvases with thick, emotional sweeps of the bright oil paints she loved so much. That was how she had navigated the emotional quagmire of her father's sudden death and the loss of her baby. With no one other than Evie in her life to turn to—and Serena hadn't ever fully opened up to her about everything she'd been through—it was still the way she dealt with the onset of any hard emotions. But since she was unable to do that, she would go to the gym in her hotel instead and exercise out her rage. Lately boxing had become her workout of choice. She would punch the bag until her hair was damp and her arms were aching and her body was rid of the frustration weighing it down.

She'd only taken a few steps, however, when she crashed into something solid and, with a yelp of surprise, stumbled backwards. It was only the sudden grip of a strong arm around her waist preventing her from toppling backwards that made her realise it was a *someone* that she had crashed into.

'Oh, my goodness, I am so sorry. I wasn't focusing on where I was going and I...' As Serena lifted her head, the collision of her gaze with a set of smooth silvery-grey eyes drove the words she had been about to speak right out of her mind.

Her body quaked with the immediate attraction that pulsed sharp and hot behind her breastbone, and she found herself unable to stop the spread of pleasant heat across her cheeks. Powerless to do anything except stare up at the owner of those mesmerising eyes and as her gaze clung to his impressive features, her heart chimed once, twice, three times. Each strike was more forceful than the last, because he was without question, the most devastatingly sexy man she had ever set eyes upon.

The cut of his face was sharp and distinct and his chiselled features were tanned. His jaw was strong without being square and was dusted with a light stubble that he wore with style. His hair was cut close to his head and dark brows that were straight and imposing sat above those unusual, intriguing eyes of the softest grey. And Serena was intrigued, in a way she had not been in an awfully long time, and in a way that was threatening to set her ablaze right then and there.

There was a small siren of warning somewhere in her brain, instructing her to look away or, even better, to walk away, but she couldn't summon the necessary willpower to do either. And then he flashed a smile that had even more plumes of desire unfurling in her stomach. 'It's fine. I probably wasn't paying as much attention as I should have been to where I was walking either.'

As his accent—South African? Australian?—brushed across her senses and stirred them into an even more heightened state of awareness, Serena felt more colour bloom in her cheeks. It startled her, that heady rush of attraction for the second time in less than a minute because it had been so long since she'd felt anything that even remotely resembled desire, and she knew she really should look away before it wrote itself even more blatantly across her face and she thoroughly embarrassed herself. Only she couldn't. Because he was staring back at her just as intently and his magnetising gaze was holding her captive.

'That's kind of you to say, but I think we both know it was my fault,' she breathed out in a rush, as the heat clamouring beneath her skin intensified. 'Are you sure I didn't hurt you?'

'No damage at all.' His gaze made a quick yet thorough sweep over her face and he immediately spoke again. 'But I'd be happy to invent some minor injury as a pretext for you to stick around a little while longer.'

The irreverent suggestion had a smile tugging at Serena's lips. 'That would be a pretty shameless thing to do, don't you think?'

'Without a doubt.' His gaze grew even livelier, sparkling with a rich masculine appreciation that made Serena's breath catch and her pulse quicken. She couldn't remember the last time a member of the opposite sex had looked at her like that. She certainly hadn't been looking for it and would probably have run a mile had anyone shown a real interest, but every now and then that little boost to her confidence would have been welcome. Because underneath all of Marcia's rules it had been hard not to feel like she was fading, becoming invisible. Every time a set of eyes had bypassed her in her dark clothes and sparsely made-up face and locked onto Evie or one of the other girls, she'd felt it that bit more. But he was seeing her and liking what he saw. And that was more powerful, more disarming that she would have expected. 'But I don't mind engaging in some shameless behaviour every now and then, especially if it helps me to get what I want,' he confessed with a quirk of his lips that sent a charge zipping along her spine and made her wonder exactly what else his lips could do and how they would feel moving over her skin. The musing was as shocking as the warm ripples that moved through her in helpless response to it.

'And what is it that you want?' she asked, the flirtatious riposte falling from her lips before she could stop it.

Her heart rapped out another beat of warning, not that Serena needed it. She could feel herself edging closer to the dangerous territory that she normally avoided at all costs, but she couldn't seem to stop herself. Something about him was pulling her further and further in, encouraging everything she knew she shouldn't be feeling. Everything she hadn't wanted to feel since suffering her miscarriage, because she knew exactly where those feelings led. To pleasure, but also, potentially, to pain.

The worst pain she'd ever known and never wanted to experience again.

'What I want,' he began, and his eyes as they swept over her again, were hot—shameless and decadent, 'is for you to have a drink with me.'

The thrill that streaked through her sent her pulse beating desperately against her skin, but she shook her head quickly, before her traitorous lips could strike again. 'I can't.'

'You can't?' His eyebrows arched, taken aback by her words. And she wasn't surprised. There was an aura of power about him, which suggested that he was unaccustomed to hearing the word *no* from anyone—in either a personal or professional capacity—but most especially from women.

She gave another shake of her head, her throat growing dry. 'I was actually just leaving to go back to my hotel. I had dinner with my friends and they headed into the club, but I have an early start. My boss likes a rundown of her daily schedule first thing in the morning and...'

He moved a step closer and Serena instantly fell silent. Her body started to hum as his grey eyes glowed down at her, glittering as if they'd been made from stardust. Their bodies were almost touching again, his tall and lean physique just a fingertip away, and she could detect the scent of his skin; hints of lemon and vanilla dancing beneath her nose, forcing her to take only the tiniest of breaths even though she wanted to take a deep inhale of him, to catch that scent and hold it close. Drown in it. 'One drink. I promise not to keep you out too late.'

Serena's throat dried even more, and the lowest part of her stomach tightened too, because that wasn't the only promise glittering in his eyes. There was heat and seduction swirling in them too and, God help her, Serena wanted to say yes. More than she'd ever wanted to say yes to anything.

It wasn't just that he was making her feel more than she'd felt in a long time, he was making her feel as she'd never felt before, all fizzed up inside like a shaken bottle of champagne. And she wanted more if it. She wanted more of this intoxicating and vibrant sense of being alive, of being on the edge of something unknown and exciting. She wanted to feel more of the delicious, dangerous heat that unravelled within her when his smoky eyes swept over her, more of the fierce beating of her pulse, the way he was making her feel beautiful and sexy and wanted when she so often felt the complete opposite.

But the consequences...

Drinks with handsome men with wicked smiles and sexy eyes were even more forbidden than nightclubs and short skirts, and should she find out, Marcia wouldn't hesitate to exact her punishment, and that awareness had Serena's heart fluttering fretfully. But even more frightening was the risk she'd be taking with her own body and heart if she did leap into that fire, as part of her very much wanted to. She had her own reasons for avoiding intimacy of any kind—because she didn't want to risk falling pregnant again. Even the thought of it was enough to crack her heart apart, and it was that fear which flowed through her blood, intensifying with every second.

The only thing Serena could do, what she *had* to do,

was repeat her refusal. But then she imagined her handsome stranger tuning away and disappearing from her sight forever. A sense of lung-squeezing loss gripped her, and she knew that she couldn't say no.

Would there really be any harm in one drink with him? In letting herself, for a little while, enjoy an exhilarating flirtation with a very handsome man? It didn't need to go any further than that. And she was seven thousand miles away from home, after all. There was no reason for Marcia to ever know it happened. But Serena would. It would a be a break from her normal monotony, a delicious memory to tuck away and take out to look at on her loneliest and dreariest days, of which there were many.

'Alright, one drink,' she agreed, fireworks exploding in her stomach as she seized the moment and chose to forget, just this once and just for a little while, the many reasons why she absolutely shouldn't.

The first thought in Caleb Morgenthau's head when he looked down at the woman who had crashed into him was that she was beautiful. With red-gold hair falling in a gleaming wave down her back and the creamy complexion of her slender face that boasted prominent cheekbones and bright eyes, she was captivating. His second thought was to wonder if she had walked into him on purpose. He'd known women to do far crazier things to get his attention. His third thought, hot on the heels of his second, was that he didn't really care whether the collision had been a construct on her part or an accident. The result remained the same. He was interested. Very much so. But having learned from past mistakes, Caleb was careful to only engage with women who had a similar mindset as his own, women uninterested in anything other than a night of pleasurable abandon, and before he took things any further, he needed to make sure she fit that mould.

He studied her with an assessing gaze and, reading the heat in the eyes that clung to him and sensing the same hunger for a night of uncomplicated pleasure beating through her blood, Caleb, to his delight, intuited there was no danger at all in indulging his temptation and invited her to join him for a drink. Her initial refusal didn't concern him—he'd never felt in any real danger of being rejected—and now he was leading her up to the rooftop lounge, where they would linger for one drink, maybe two, before hopefully ending the evening in his bed.

His mind was already racing ahead to that moment when he could slide the dress from her body and see the delights that lay beneath. He could picture her long red hair spilling across his pillows, her creamy skin glowing beneath the white fire of the moonlight as she stared up at him with breathless rapture while he brought her to orgasm over and over again. The sexy image had an irresistible anticipation roaring through his veins, unlike anything he'd felt for the longest time.

When was the last time he'd been so impatient for a woman? Lately his sexual encounters had become indistinguishable from one another, the experiences all shades of the same colour. But there was something about this woman whose name he didn't yet know. Something about the way her eyes had held his, how that slow curving smile seemed to hint at something different. Something unexpected. He felt drawn to her in a way he couldn't put words to.

He was so deep in his musings that it was only her small gasp of delight as they emerged on the rooftop that alerted him to their arrival.

'Wow. I thought the city was beautiful from down on the ground, but from here it's even more spectacular.' Her eyes swept side to side several times to take in the wonder of Singapore's glowing skyline; the pale lights of the business district and the colourful illuminations of the Gardens by the Bay. 'I'm surprised it's not busier up here though,' she commented, as he led her to a vacant table in the corner with views across the vibrant city. 'I thought the rooftop lounge was fully booked tonight. My friend, Evie, wanted to come up here for a drink before dinner and was so disappointed when we couldn't get in.'

'This is the members-only rooftop lounge,' Caleb informed her as a waiter arrived at their table with two flutes of champagne, depositing one in front of each of them. 'It's solely for VIP guests.'

Her eyes went round with surprise, looking first at him and then around the intimately lit surroundings. The tables were well spaced out, and many of them were occupied with parties of varying sizes. He watched her eyes pop with shocked recognition as she spotted the cluster of Hollywood superstars sitting with minor members of the British Royal Family and then graze the world-renowned tennis champion at the table behind, celebrating his latest championship title.

'Well, I certainly feel foolish for not having realised

that before now.' She reached for her glass and was half-way to lifting it to her full pink lips when she froze, her eyes turning back to him. 'That makes you a VIP guest too?'

'Technically I'm the owner.' He held out his hand, seeing further surprise abound through her expression. 'Caleb Morgenthau.'

It was a novel experience for him to not be known. In Australia, the Morgenthau name was widely recognised, and as the son of such a professionally prominent and socially powerful father, Caleb's profile had always been high. His personal business success, along with his unattainable, untameable bachelor status, had generated even greater attention around him, attention that followed him wherever he went, and six months of living in Singapore hadn't changed that. He knew women were often drawn to him because of that notoriety. It didn't bother him. He wasn't looking for anything to last longer than a night, so the motives of the women who sought him out were immaterial, but it was refreshing to know that it hadn't played any part in her interest and that she was there for the same reasons as him—pure physical and sexual attraction.

Slowly, almost shyly, she slid her fingers against his, and the feeling of her soft, delicate hand encased in his had the strongest sensations rippling across his skin. Her skin was as smooth and warm as he had imagined and the desire to touch more of her flared through him like a rocket, because her hand fit so seamlessly inside of his that he knew their bodies would lock together just as perfectly, as if they were connecting pieces of a jigsaw puzzle. 'Serena Addison.'

Beneath his fingertips her pulse fluttered at twice the normal speed and that same explosion of feeling was mirrored in the eyes that boldly held his gaze.

'Serena,' he repeated, liking how the syllables rolled around his mouth. It was a name he wanted to say again and again and again. 'That's beautiful. It suits you.'

'Thank you.' Their eyes continued to hold in a way that had Caleb's blood thickening and a series of low throbs beating pleasantly in his groin. 'My mother was Italian, and even though she married an Englishman and settled in England, she wanted to honour her heritage with the name that she gave me.'

As Serena spoke, she rearranged her legs in front of her, drawing Caleb's eyes down to their spectacular slim shape and length, and he couldn't keep himself from imagining them curled around his waist. They were the only part of her body that her silky navy dress showcased, but she was definitely right to show them off. It took a giant surge of willpower to angle his gaze away from them quickly.

'Italian?' he asked, reaching for his own glass and taking a sip to moisten his mouth, because even by his standards, it was too soon to start taking it further yet. 'Do you spend much time in Italy?'

She gave a light shake of her head. 'No. I haven't been there in a long time.'

'How come?'

'There aren't many reasons to. My mother left the country because she had didn't have any family left there and wanted a fresh start. We used to visit when I was younger, but she passed away when I was twelve and I've never been back.'

She made that final admission quickly, as though it caused her physical pain to speak that fact aloud, and Caleb could hear her sadness and the loss she felt. It changed the tenor of her voice, momentarily casting a shadow across her beautiful face, and he found himself longing to reach out and smooth it away, which surprised him as he wasn't usually given to such tender impulses. But he was familiar with the deep ache of not having a mother. For Serena, however, to have lost her mother after knowing her and being loved by her…well, that was a cruelty he couldn't speak to. His mother had absconded before Caleb could even begin to remember her, and a person couldn't miss what they'd never had, could they? At least, that was what he always told himself in the moments he caught himself approaching some form of pathetic, melancholic sentimentality.

'It's a shame that you lost her at such a young age,' Caleb sympathised, focusing on Serena instead of the dart of poisonous feeling arrowing across his chest that accompanied any consideration of the woman who'd given him life. The woman whose decision to leave and never return had carved a void in him that had never been filled and created a wedge between him and his father that was yet to be bridged.

'It is. She was a very vibrant character and a lot of fun, so her loss left a big void.' Sadness haunted the rim of her eyes as she continued, 'But it's much worse for my younger brother and sister. They never even had the chance to know her. I, at least, have my memories.' Her eyes grew wet and she blinked rapidly, angling her face away. 'I'm sorry. I don't know why I'm getting emotional. This is terrible drinks conversation.'

'It's fine conversation.' Gently placing a finger under her chin, he turned her face back to his, but the sparks that ignited from that brief moment of contact seemed to still them both, their gazes meeting and holding, the air seeming to charge as they did. 'You have nothing to apologise for.'

With a swipe of her inky lashes, she banished the sadness from her eyes and smiled again, a smile of determination. 'Your turn now, Caleb Morgenthau. Tell me about you,' she invited, leaning her head on her hand and looking at him through such bright eyes and with such a soft smile that he was captivated all over again, and he found himself leaning in to her as close as possible, as if being pulled by some invisible thread.

'What would you like to know?'

'You're Australian, yes?' At his nod of confirmation, she smiled. 'Whereabouts in Australia is home?'

'I was born and raised in Melbourne, but nowadays home is wherever I'm establishing a new venue. In the last few years, I've lived in Sydney, Bali, Hong Kong and here in Singapore.'

'You have places like this in all those cities?' she asked, looking more than a little impressed.

'Not exactly like this, but yes. And few more besides.' Caleb grinned. 'Now that this place is running successfully and there's a good management team in place, the next stop is Europe. After that, the plan is to expand into North America.'

'So, you're looking to conquer the world?'

'Perhaps I am.' He smiled, but in that moment, he was far more interested in conquering her. Taking her over kiss by kiss, touch by touch, until she was completely and undeniably his.

The smile dancing at the corners of her mouth made him think she knew exactly what he was thinking, that she was thinking it too. She took another sip of her champagne. 'Where are you opening in Europe?'

'Saint-Tropez. Mykonos. Rome and London,' he answered, waiting for the hint to be dropped that she would love to visit those venues and pleasantly surprised when it didn't. Usually, the women he met couldn't wait to exploit the connection for access to his luxurious nightlife experiences.

Instead, her eyes shone. 'You're so lucky. Getting to live and work in all those different places.' Wistfulness infused her words and made him think of his younger self, of the days that he'd spent chafing at the ties that bound him, dreaming of an escape, of freedom, and he wondered what it was that she was dreaming of escaping. Responsibilities at home perhaps? She had mentioned having younger siblings. 'Was this what you always wanted to do?'

'I wouldn't exactly say that,' he admitted with a wry smile. 'It's an inherited family business. My grandfather owned a small restaurant in Melbourne fifty years ago. My father joined the business at sixteen and when he eventually took over, he expanded across the state. By the time I was growing up, we had places in every major city across Australia and it was just expected that I would join the business and one day take over. I was never asked if it was what I wanted to do, and I struggled with that choice of how I wanted to live my life being essentially taken from me. I felt…' Caleb searched for the best way to describe it, even though he had never been good at drawing feelings out of himself or putting his emotions into words. He had figured out at a young age that it was better to bury whatever he felt, rather than be consumed by it.

'Boxed in,' Serena supplied knowingly, and it took him aback that she could so easily identify what he had felt. As if she too knew that feeling. As if they were connected.

'Yes. Exactly,' he breathed, staring at her with a strange lump forming in his throat, because when had he ever felt such a strong bond of kindship with anyone else, especially a woman?

Was that what had compelled him to share so much in that moment, when expressing his feelings quite so openly about anything wasn't something he ever did. He was certainly asked his fair share of probing questions, but Caleb always denied the requests to drill into his life, holding everyone, especially women, at arm's length. Life, he'd learned, was safer that way. Tidier.

'I get it. Having your life mapped out for you before you have the chance to claim it as your own is not easy.' Something moved in her eyes that told of her own experience with that, and he felt his breath catch again, the same strange feeling hooking in his chest. 'But you obviously managed to get past it somehow?'

'Eventually I realised I was lucky to be part of something, to be part of that legacy and that it was time I started contributing to it. And I knew how much it meant to my father too, to have me be part of it.'

'Both he and your grandfather must be incredibly proud of all you're achieving.'

'I think my father would be happier if I slowed down long enough to have a family and provide the next generation of Morgenthaus, but since that's not going to happen, he'll have to be content with global expansion.'

Caleb couldn't fathom where those words had come from either, other than his earlier conversation with his father was still playing on his mind. It was the same discussion they'd had a dozen times already—his father exerting paternal pressure on him to fulfil the rest of his obligation and provide heirs to continue the family legacy—and it had ended the same as every other time, in a stony stalemate. His father didn't want to hear his refusals, and Caleb wasn't willing to offer the reasoning behind his unyielding stance. The events, scorched into his brain, were not moments of his life he had any interest in talking about, especially not with his father. They had never been close like that, not after his father had spent the majority of Caleb's formative years battling his heartache over his wife's desertion and finding solace in burying himself in work and never in his son—the son he held responsible for that loss.

'You're don't plan on getting married and having a family?' Serena queried.

'No. I like my life as it is. I have no desire to change it,' he answered, with a frankness that left no room for doubt. He liked to always have those cards face up on the table so any woman who crossed his path knew what to expect. And what *not* to expect. That was key. Not that it was necessary, not when he was so careful to only entertain women on the same page as him. 'Now, I think it's your turn again,' Caleb said, his eyes mapping the striking planes of her face. 'Tell me what brought you to Singapore?'

'Work. My boss is looking to expand her overseas business, so we're here, taking lots of meetings and exploring new opportunities.'

'Do you like your job?'

She nodded impassively. 'I've been doing it for a few years.'

He smiled, recognising avoidance when he saw it. 'That isn't what I asked.'

She sighed, funnelling her fingers through her hair and releasing the sweetest scent into the air between them. It quickened Caleb's heart and caused his pulse to thud with even more eagerness. He wanted to bury his face in that scent, in her neck and her hair. 'If you're asking if I dreamed of being an executive assistant as a little girl, then no.'

'Why didn't you pursue your dream?' She didn't seem like someone lacking in courage or confidence, so he was curious as to why she had settled for something she didn't want.

More curiosity, Caleb. Really?

It was unusual for him, he had to admit, but he couldn't help it.

A sadness, or perhaps a weariness, came into her eyes,

and she momentarily turned her gaze away, looking off into the starry sky. 'I kind of got boxed in too.' It was then that he saw it flash in her eyes, everything he had once felt. The constraint, the powerlessness, the frustration.

'By what?'

She shook her head gently. 'It's really too long of a story to go into,' she murmured, drawing her eyes down and away from his, and when she looked back at him, they had shuttered, and he didn't like that at all. 'And I think it's time I should be going anyway.'

The words caught him off guard. She wanted to leave? 'You should?'

'Yes. I said one drink and that drink is finished. Thank you. It was nice meeting you, Caleb.'

Caleb stared at her as she got to her feet, a slight frown pinching between his brows. Women had walked away from him before. Not often, but it had happened. He'd never been all that bothered. There were always other women. But he was bothered now, watching her prepare to leave with a rapidly beating heart. Because she was beautiful and he wanted to take her, yes. But, also, because he wanted to know more of her. Because the past while with her was the most connected he'd felt to another person in a long time. It wasn't a feeling Caleb had been seeking, or that he had ever sought, nor was it something that he'd particularly felt he was missing because he knew the chaos that emotional connections caused. Yet in spite of how strange it felt pulsing within his chest and how worryingly out of character that was, he wasn't ready to let it go.

And where was the harm in indulging it for a little while longer? It wouldn't linger. His interest never did.

'Are you sure you can't stay another while?'

Serena swallowed the emotion at the back of her throat. Was she sure? No, she wasn't.

She knew she couldn't stay, that she needed to leave. Not just because of Marcia, but because the more they talked and shared and the longer she lingered in his sphere of dominance, spellbound by his glittering eyes and undeniable charm, the greater was the temptation to throw caution to the wind, let all else drift from her mind and into the starry stratosphere above and give in to what she wanted.

Him.

To let herself, for one night, be and feel without restraint. Without *fear*. Her defences had already melted away and she could feel the tendrils of temptation stroking, beckoning. She was only a single step away from crossing that all-important line and diving head first into reckless abandon, and goodness knew where that would lead her this time. It wasn't as though Caleb was offering anything; on the contrary, he'd made it clear he wasn't looking for anything serious or permanent. It was a risk that she just couldn't take. So, leaving was imperative.

Yet the compulsion to stay was just as strong. Every cell in her body longed to sit back down and bask under his attention, the delight of being seen and considered. Being visible. And it wasn't as though Serena wanted a promise of something more, or would even believe it if one was made, not with the memory of Lucas's flimsy promises still strong in her mind. But she did want Caleb, and whatever sense and strength she had found to stick to her original promise of leaving after one drink was fading under that beseeching look in his eyes that whispered her agreeing to stay would make his every dream come true.

She'd never felt so torn in two, as if there was no wrong answer, rightness in both choices, staying and leaving.

'I'm sure,' she said on a deep breath, feeling the crash of relief and disappointment.

He nodded, something that looked a lot like disappointment flaring in his eyes. Seeing how he felt about her, when he could have any woman he wanted, made her heart sigh. 'I'll come down to the lobby with you. Arrange a car to take you back to your hotel.'

Serena waved away the offer, certain than every extra second spent with this man was a moment that threatened to change her mind. 'You don't need to do that.'

'I want to,' he insisted, placing a hand at the small of her back as he walked her towards the elevator. He wasn't actually touching her and yet Serena's skin burned as if he was. *Imagine how good it would feel if he did actually touch you.* She chased the dangerous thought from her mind. She'd made her decision, the safe and smart one. 'You're alone and don't know your way around the city, and I'll spend all night worrying about you otherwise.'

Serena quite liked the thought of him spending all night dwelling on her. It would mean she wasn't alone in brooding over him, because she knew that was what was going to happen. She would relive her encounter with him over again, fall asleep dreaming of him, dreams that would no doubt leave her hot and achy.

'If you insist,' she acquiesced, praying the ride down would be fast because her mind was already starting to swim with the potency of his scent.

But as they stepped inside, it was even worse than she had feared. Trapped in such a small, enclosed space, with the scent of him infusing every breath she took, her heart went berserk. Racing. Leaping. *Wanting*. Serena fixed her eyes to the floor, reminding herself of all the reasons why she couldn't. Mustn't. But the heat bubbling beneath her skin continued to soar because he was so close, close enough that she could reach out and touch him.

Suddenly the lights flickered and the car jolted so violently that Serena lost her balance and tumbled into Caleb. He caught her, preventing her from falling any further with the solid wall of his chest and by securing his arms around her waist. His hold tightened as they jolted again, and this time Serena couldn't keep the gasp of alarm from squeaking from her mouth. Caleb pulled her even more securely against his body.

The lights snapped back on and the car steadied. Still holding her, Caleb looked down at her, concern written across his face. 'Are you OK?'

She nodded, her heart in her throat. 'Yes. What was that?'

'A power surge, most likely. Are you sure you're OK?'

She could only nod, words deserting her again as those silver eyes glowed down at her and she became aware that the throb of fear that her life was going to end was ebbing away and being replaced by a different, more pleasant and intoxicating throb, emanating from where his fingers were warm and firm against her body. Her heart rapped out a fast tattoo of warning. *Tell him he can let go of you now.* But Serena's lips wouldn't move, and the words wouldn't materialise. Because she didn't, in her heart, want him to let her go. She liked how it felt being held in his arms, liked the heady vibration of her heart and her blood. All of the feeling that had been jostling in her begged for release even more desperately and before she was even really aware of what she was doing, before she could summon the sense or power to stop herself, Serena was pressing to her tiptoes and reaching for his mouth. *Just one kiss*, she promised herself, *just so I know how it feels, and then I'll stop.*

One kiss, however, was all it took to ignite an even more ferocious fire in her blood. The press of Caleb's mouth vibrated through her whole body, unlocking the bars around those feelings so they flowed free and unchecked for the first time in so, so long—rivulets of pure, potent, sparkling sensation streaming upwards and outwards and in every other direction as he kissed her back with such exquisite tenderness and skill that Serena thought she might die of pleasure. *And wouldn't that be a perfect way to go*, she thought, feeling so replete and yet hungry for so much more that she consented to a second swipe of his lips, and then another, and by that time she was sliding her arms up to loop around his neck, securing herself to him, and any thought of stopping was obliterated from her mind entirely.

CHAPTER TWO

SERENA'S MOUTH TASTED even better than he'd thought it would. Sweet, like honey. So sweet it was quickly becoming addictive, and Caleb knew that for the rest of his life he'd never again be able to enjoy the nectar without thinking of her and that moment, the eagerness of her mouth beneath his and her yielding body.

Her lips parted beneath his and he didn't waste a second seizing that opportunity to slide his tongue into the wet heat of her mouth and back her up against the wall of the elevator. The spread of heat through his body, sure and sexy, inflamed in intensity, and sent a heavy beat drumming through his blood. Kissing her, being kissed by her was the most pleasurable assault he'd ever known, and for all that Caleb was used to this interplay between male and female—the warm scent of a woman's skin, the soft noises of assent and delight, the press of the feminine shape—with her it all felt new. Thrilling. A dream he wanted to sink even deeper into.

Maybe it was the way she responded to each sweep of his hands, as if his touch was electrifying her. Or maybe it was the way her shape fitted so sleekly against his, as though their bodies had been cut from a shared mould. Destined for one another.

It was a ridiculous thought, and not one that he would have countenanced in any other moment, but right then and there, being driven crazy by the duelling desires to savour and devour her, it seemed to make perfect sense, to explain this new vortex of sexual potency he was being sucked into. Serena was his match, her body made explicitly for his, designed to draw from him all that he could offer and to receive a pleasure that only he could deliver.

Trailing a line of fire down her neck, Caleb didn't stop until he located the spot of her hammering pulse. As he settled his mouth on that spot, the taste of her skin driving him as high as the play of his lips was sending her, that scorching convergence wound a new blistering heat around them, binding them together even more strongly.

Lifting her leg, she curled it around his thigh, and his erection, already painfully tight, throbbed at the explicit invitation, at how beautifully his pelvis nestled against the heart of her. Caleb responded instinctively, pressing even harder against her and, driven by the need to feel all of her, to take her to the highest possible peak of pleasure, slid his hand along the smooth skin of her thigh. Eager to see her bright eyes shatter with delight, to see her pleasure wash over her, his fingers ventured higher until the slight quiver of her flesh stirred an awareness that should have surfaced prior to that moment.

Because whilst he was in no doubt as to what he wanted, could Serena say the same? Mere moments ago, she'd been set on leaving, and had the jolt of the elevator not thrown her into his arms, she'd likely already be gone. And he would have let her go. He'd never had to plead with a woman to go to bed with him and never would. Nor was he a man who'd take advantage of a woman who was carried away.

'What is it? What's wrong?' she asked, her lips beautifully swollen and hair mussed from where his hands had tangled in its glossy lengths.

'Nothing. You're perfect,' he said quickly to erase that flash of insecurity in her eyes. 'And I would gladly whisk you to my suite to continue this, but I don't want you to feel that has to happen. You can still leave. I want you to be sure this is what you want too.'

Her hands were resting against his jacket, and as she smiled, they curled into the fabric, ready to pull him closer. 'I'm sure,' she replied quickly.

Too quickly? But whilst a sense continued to whisper through his mind that perhaps he should put a stop to it anyway, his body was more than convinced, his hand swiping the control panel with his access card to get them to his suite as his mouth reclaimed hers with a hunger that continued to transcend all he had ever felt before. A want that was feeling more and more like need.

Compelling, desperate, irresistible, insatiable need.

Serena was relieved when Caleb lifted her into his arms and carried her from the elevator, because she didn't know how much longer she'd be able to remain standing upright, not when every single inch of her body was trembling. Every touch, every kiss was penetrating so deeply, if felt as if her soul was shaking too.

He had asked her if she was sure, and with feeling as

powerful as that, snaking and curling through her, how could she be anything but sure?

Her world had narrowed to him, to the feelings he'd set spinning inside her. The life she had known before this evening, before him, had faded, retreating from her mind almost entirely, pushed aside to make room for all this glorious newness. She knew, however, that she had never done anything like this before, never been tempted into being ravished in an elevator, to letting a man she hadn't known before that night slide his hand between her legs. But that didn't seem to matter. There was no longer a single doubt in her heart or her head. Any reservations had been burned away by the fire blazing between them, and for this one night she would ignore what she should do and do what she wanted. Take what she craved. Needed.

There would be slowing, no stopping. She wanted the opposite. She wanted more.

As if reading that wish, Caleb's kisses grew less restrained—not that they had been restrained before—but as he lowered her to the bed, pressing her back into the covers with his weight, it was as if there was a new urgency driving him. An even deeper hunger opening up inside of him.

Serena felt it too; her body was achy and hot and only growing hotter. Restless. She'd never known a feeling like it, a desperation so pure she wasn't sure how she could stand it. Her hands went to his chest, her fingers scrabbling with the tiny buttons of his shirt, impatient to bare the hard chest beneath, and she felt his lips curve at her hurried fumbling, enjoying it. His hands were far more skilled, pushing up her dress, curling into the thin band of her knickers and sliding them down her legs to the floor in one easy move.

If there was a moment for Serena to be beset by any kind of uncertainty or hesitation, that was probably it, but, for one of the only times in her whole life, she was being ruled by impulse and impulse alone. She was trapped in the eye of a wild, heady storm, and it felt exactly right. This moment, this place, this man. It felt more right than anything had in a long time. Perhaps ever.

Locating the hidden fastening on her dress, Caleb nudged the fabric apart, a hiss emerging from between his teeth as first his eyes and then his mouth made contact with her breasts. He kissed the top of them, before dragging one lacy cup down and fastening his mouth around the nipple, laving it with his tongue until she was arching beneath him.

Nothing had ever come close to what he was making her feel, and Serena throbbed with all the glorious, pounding sensations, a restless tattoo inside her that she had never experienced before but could suddenly feel everywhere, and she arched upwards again, pressing against him.

Seeming to know exactly what she was asking for, exactly where and how she needed to be caressed, Caleb slipped his hand between their bodies, sending his fingers straight to the pulsing heart of her. That first stroke of his finger to the taut cluster of nerves zagged through her like lightning, jolting her, blinding her. Even as she cried out, he didn't stop, touching her with the perfect amount of pressure to undo her even further. He whispered words to her, words she didn't hear as she rose and fell with the ministrations of his hand, her breath so close to dying altogether. And then she was crying out again, whispering his name, begging him to stop and not stop in the same breath, as her body was rocked by one long explosion.

Immediately she wanted more. She reached for his trousers, unfastening them, and together she and Caleb pushed them down his legs. For a second, she allowed her eyes to indulge in the beauty of his naked body, but only for a second, because her hunger was too relentless to be paused for long.

'Do you have a condom?' she gasped, and he nodded surely, having already reached for his wallet from the floor. Tearing open the small foil packet with his teeth, he rolled it along his length, his hands not entirely steady, and Serena was so filled with anticipation she could barely breathe.

He covered her again, the eyes holding hers alight with pewter sparks as he nudged her entrance. That brief flicker of contact had her arching, ready to accept him, and as she did, Caleb thrust smoothly into her. Whatever tightness or strangeness there was lasted only the barest of seconds before she was filled with an overpowering sense of completion and connection. Caleb growled out a noise of contentment, shuddering from deep within his chest, and it was enormously gratifying that it felt as good for him as it did for her.

With each thrust he seemed to take pride in taking even deeper possession of her, drawing out each movement to maximise every drop of pleasure and to send the sweetness surging to the tips of her extremities.

With every thought that she was capable of, which wasn't much, Serena thought it couldn't get any better, only it did. As he hitched her leg up to lock around his waist and claimed her lips, he drove into her with a surge of such desire that her hands clawed down his back, needing to remain anchored to something because she could feel everything—her sense of self and life—shattering around her. And then she was gone, soaring past pleasure, past sanity, past all she'd believed was possible and landing in the abyss. Only it wasn't dark and lonely; it was a bright, sparkling land where pleasure followed pleasure and for the longest time she drifted, floating amongst those beautiful, starry sensations.

But then those quakes of delight began to ebb away and the stars started to fade and everything that had been shunted aside by the needy impulses that had flowered so powerfully, so violently, inside of her, rushed back.

Slowly, so slowly it felt a hundred times worse, it dawned on her the risks she had taken, the jeopardy she had put herself in, her body and her heart. It settled over her like a chill. Horror bottlenecked her throat, and the thuds of her heart echoed like crashes of doom.

There was only one thing she could do, and it was what she should have done long before now—get out of there as fast as she could.

Caleb was still riding the wave, his breath burning his lungs and his body feeling as though it had been struck by a supercharged bolt of lightning. He'd always enjoyed sex but nothing before had ever come close to that. He wanted to savour it, bask in each and every sensation rippling through his body, but he was also greedy to start all over again. The night was long, but nowhere near long enough for him to enjoy and explore Serena in all the ways he was already vividly—very vividly—imagining before they had to go their separate ways.

Feeling the mattress shift, he turned his head to the side, frowning when he saw that she was sitting up and covering her lovely body with her dress.

'Are you OK?'

'Yes,' she replied, too fast and in an octave too high for her voice, so that he was instantly alert. 'I just need to leave.'

'Is something wrong?' Concern launched him into a sitting position so he could see her better.

'No. I just… I should get back to my hotel. I shouldn't be here.' Those words sounded all wrong, especially as it was his view that she was exactly where she should be and where he wanted her to spend the rest of the night. He was on the verge of reaching out to her when she bolted off the bed, practically running to the door of his bedroom without looking at him once, and he was sure he heard her say *I shouldn't have done this.*

'Serena?' he called after her, his chest thumping hard with emotion he couldn't fully comprehend.

His brain whirring with confusion, Caleb searched the floor. Locating his trousers where they'd been hastily discarded, he pulled them on and followed her into the suites living space, where she located her bag and then turned so hastily for the elevator that she nearly knocked into an end table. Caleb hurried to intercept her, catching her arm. 'Serena, stop.'

He spun her around to face him, and as her face lifted

to his, he saw the panic darting through her eyes, but it was the unshed tears that triggered his own awareness and it hit him like a punch to the gut.

He only had one rule and he had just broken it.

He released her arm, scalded as much by the force of his own feelings as he was by the look on her face. The horror surging through his bloodstream thickened until it felt as if it would clog his veins and his lungs, even his throat. His heart pounded in his ears, a torrid drumbeat of sound before he ordered himself to take a breath, and then another, so that his voice would be somewhat steady when he spoke. Because he had to speak. He had to ask the question. As much as he didn't want to breathe any more life into this nightmare, he needed to know. 'You don't normally do anything like this, do you?' he demanded, his voice not without sympathy because he could see that she was as out of her depth as him. Just for a very different reason.

Her throat quivered. 'Anything like what?' she asked, bravely lifting her head to meet his eyes.

The answering look he sent her was piercing, but she didn't flinch. 'Going back to a hotel room with a man you just met and having sex with him?' He snapped the words out, as with each second his patience was fraying too much to keep his tone measured, and her skin turned an even paler shade of white.

She swallowed, making him wait before she answered. 'No.'

'Never?' he demanded, hoping that maybe she wasn't as innocent as his worst thoughts were telling him.

'Never,' she clarified, spitting out the word as though

it had refused to come willingly, the last thing she wanted to admit.

Her face faded from his view. All he could see was bright red flashing lights of alarm, feel panic surrounding him like cement walls closing in. He had his rules for a reason, and he abided by them for a reason. Because he didn't ever want to hurt a woman the way he had hurt Charlotte.

She hadn't been one of his usual carefree, sophisticated lovers either, but he hadn't cared about that when he'd brought her into his life. He'd wanted her and had pursued her with no thought for those differences, never thinking that perhaps their affair had greater meaning to her than it did to him. Never caring enough to find out. And he had devastated her in ways that were carved into his mind—the memories a stain that would never fade.

That was why he only engaged with women like him now, women who understood how he operated. Women who he couldn't devastate, because the only thing they wanted from him was something he was more than willing to give. Pleasure. Distraction. He had thought Serena was, or had he just wanted to believe that because of how urgently he'd wanted her from that first moment? Had the signs been there and he just hadn't wanted to acknowledge them? He feared so. He had wanted her too much. And that was unforgivable.

'You weren't...' His voice deserted him, the thought that had just occurred to him out of nowhere ripping the breath from his lungs. 'Please tell me this wasn't your first time,' he pleaded, because taking an innocent would be too much.

'What does that have to do with anything?' she demanded on a breath that managed to be both anguished and furious.

'Answer the question.'

Their gazes warred. His desperate. Hers blistering with reproach. 'No,' she finally snapped. 'I wasn't a virgin.'

'That's something at least,' he breathed, a fraction of the two-tonne weight lifting from his chest. 'But, regardless, you are right—this shouldn't have happened. You should not be here right now.' Her gaze reflected pain and anger at receiving those words, but he didn't allow himself to feel bad. She needed to understand so that she didn't walk away with any hope that this meant more than what it had been. Or that he was someone he wasn't. 'It's my fault, not yours. I should have…' *Been more careful. Stopped. Heeded my thoughts.* He should have done all of the above, but what was the use of going backwards? Nothing he said or did now could change what had happened. He had learned that lesson the hard way a long time ago. 'I'm sorry. I'll have a car pick you up downstairs and drive you back to your hotel.' What *you should have done an hour ago.*

Serena barely managed a nod, her mouth tight, her eyes focused on the floor rather than him and her arms wound tightly across her chest as she walked to the elevator. It was a desolate sight, and one that nipped at his insides for reasons that he had no interest in unravelling. 'I'm not trying to be cruel, Serena. But I don't… the women I usually take to bed are more experienced, more like me. They are as uninterested in a relationship as I am. They understand…'

She stepped hastily into the elevator as it arrived, lifting her head at last and spearing him with the sudden angry flash of her amber eyes. 'You can save the speech, Caleb. I understand perfectly well that this was just a one-night thing, and as hard as you may find it to believe, I wasn't looking for it to be anything more than a brief interlude. So, you have nothing to worry about. I get it loud and clear that you're only interested in bedding and forgetting women, and since you've already successfully completed the first part, now you can start on the forgetting part. That's exactly what I'm planning to do.'

Her words rooted him to the spot. The truth was his sexual encounters didn't take up any space in his mind, and it didn't bother him in the slightest if the women he'd slept with never thought of him again, so why did hearing Serena say that she would forget him make him clench with anger, make him want to reach out, take her in his arms and force her to take the words back? And why as the doors of the elevator slid to a soundless close and whisked her out of his life for good, was he left with the searing feeling in his chest that he was losing something, when she'd never been his to begin with?

CHAPTER THREE

SO MUCH FOR forgetting that night had ever happened,
Serena thought eight weeks later, the heavy bumps of her
heart echoing all the way up in her throat as the small
strip in the centre of the plastic white stick she held in her
trembling hand turned a bright and unmistakable pink.

She swallowed, the panic that she had so far managed to hold at bay erupting in her chest as the truth sank
through her like a chill. *Pregnant.*

She'd been feeling unwell for weeks now, but had at-
tributed it to the stomach virus running rampant through
her office. Even as those around her had recovered within
a week, Serena had clung to that explanation, willing it
to be that simple, because the thought that the universe
had dealt her the fate she most feared after a single act
of intimacy in five years was too much to bear.

She hadn't thought about that night since. She hadn't
wanted to remember the humiliation as Caleb had probed
her level of sexual history, or the sting of rejection as he'd
dismissed the night as a mistake because of her lack of
experience, and it had seemed safer to not recall how
heavenly it had felt in his arms. She had just put it from
her mind and continued on as though it hadn't happened.

But now…

Dropping her head into her hands, Serena cursed herself for stupidly believing that she could seize that one night of pleasure and not suffer any consequences. Life had never been that kind to her, and now that uncharacteristic moment of abandon had invited the past to repeat itself with a pregnancy that she was terrified to want in case it all went heartbreakingly wrong again and she was left to lament her failure once more. Because the miscarriage had to have been her fault, didn't it? Something she had done or had failed to do? That was the only option. The doctors hadn't been able to provide any other definite answer.

Serena had still been reeling from the shock of discovering that she was pregnant and the agony that her boyfriend had deserted her within twenty-four hours of learning the news, when she had miscarried. Knowing that something was wrong, that the sharp pains stabbing her stomach were abnormal but that there was nothing she could do to stop it had been excruciating. It had been one of the worst moments of her life when the sombre-faced doctor had entered the room and explained to her what was happening—having to contend with yet another loss and to do so without anyone there to support her. But like everything else she had been through, Serena had survived and it had made her stronger. Helped her to learn to stand on her own two feet and rely on herself for support and salvation. She would need all of that and more now.

She would find no grace or support from her stepmother. All she had proven was that Marcia's accusations and criticisms of impulsivity and carelessness were spot on, and more than anything that was a vindication she couldn't bear giving the older woman. But she would have to, wouldn't she? Her stepmother made it her business to know everything, and by Serena's reckoning she was nearly eight weeks pregnant. She'd thrown up every day for the past fortnight. How long before her stepmother put the pieces together? And when she did, Serena knew what would happen. Marcia had been horrified by the scandal of her first pregnancy and, fearing for her own reputation, had made it clear that Serena and her illegitimate child were not welcome in her home. This time would be no different.

For a moment Serena was paralysed by the familiar feeling of powerlessness, of life being swept out of her control again, and she had to remind herself that she wasn't a child this time, nor was she helpless. She would be fine on her own. Emotionally she'd been on her own since her father had died, but it was what it meant for Kit and Alexis that troubled her most deeply. The chances were, Marica wouldn't allow her to still see them, but perhaps Serena could sit down with her stepmother and appeal to her better nature… Oh, who was she kidding? Marcia didn't have a better nature, definitely not where Serena was concerned, and Serena knew she was partially to blame for that.

Although it had been over two years since her mother's passing when her father introduced Marcia, Serena had struggled with having a new woman in their lives, especially one so different from her mother. It hadn't helped that whilst Marcia had made every effort to bond with the twins, her treatment of Serena had been more lukewarm. Serena had realised why when she overhead Marcia talking to her friends, lamenting how closely Serena resembled her mother and how difficult she found that. Her father had insisted that with time they would get used to one another, but time didn't make things easier. Serena's struggle only intensified once they married and Marcia adopted the twins—a fate she flatly refused for herself—and it seemed that making room for Marcia in their lives meant erasing nearly all trace of her mother. It was only through the refereeing of her father that their relationship remained relatively peaceful, but once he was gone there'd been nothing to temper their resentment of each other, and relations had deteriorated quickly. Had it not meant leaving Kit and Alexis behind, she would have left and not looked back, but walking away from them was unthinkable.

Only now she was facing exactly that.

As hard as Serena looked, she could see no way to keep it from happening. The only way would be to quickly and quietly terminate the pregnancy, but Serena recoiled from that thought as soon as it formed.

She may be terrified, but she wanted her baby.

It wasn't what she'd planned—she hadn't been sure she'd ever want to try for a child again after what happened last time—but there was no question how precious the little life nestled inside of her was. Her only wish was that it didn't have to upend everything else and once again she cursed herself for getting so carried away by Caleb's touch…

Caleb.

His name reverberated through her like a punch. She'd been so preoccupied with the consequences closer to home that she hadn't even considered him, but of course she would have to tell him about the pregnancy. He had every right to know. Only the thought of sharing that news with him sent her blood pressure skyrocketing, because how was she supposed to tell a man she'd only met once that their passionate encounter had resulted in a baby? A man who had been very clear that he had zero desire for a family or to make a commitment longer than a night to anyone.

A man who had made it clear that he regretted making love to her at all.

That shouldn't have happened. You should not be here right now.

The brutal words sounded in her mind, bringing the sting of tears to her eyes and causing her stomach to lurch with the same violent rejection she'd felt in his suite, the very same feeling as when she'd realised Lucas had deserted her. Would Caleb tell her that the child they'd created was a mistake also? That thought made her angry enough to do something she would never have expected and question if she needed to tell him at all. She hadn't hesitated all those years ago to tell Lucas that she was pregnant, but he'd been her boyfriend. She'd thought they were in love and would weather everything together; never had she anticipated that he would run from her and his responsibilities.

Caleb Morgenthau was another story. She had no reason to expect him to be pleased about the news. Wouldn't it be a kindness to spare herself another brutal rejection?

Or the crushing disappointment of another man making it blindingly clear he had no interest in the child he fathered? Never mind that the worst could happen still and it would all be for nothing...but no, that wasn't a possibility that Serena would give any willing headspace to. She would think positive thoughts only. The doctor at the time had reassured her that there was no reason to believe she wouldn't conceive and carry successfully in the future, and she really wanted to believe that.

As for telling Caleb, it was the right thing to do. She'd never be able to face herself in the mirror again if she didn't. After scouring the internet, she located a public email address on his website and composed an email. Serena was surprised at how easily the words came and how few were needed to share the news. But she wasn't asking him for anything, so that made it straightforward. Hitting Send, she turned off the laptop and sank onto her bed, seeing no reason to wait for a response because there wasn't a single part of her that expected one. Not after seeing all the tabloid gossip surrounding Caleb online, referring to him as Australia's Untameable Bachelor and documenting the exploits that never included the same woman twice.

After Lucas left the way he did, Serena had sworn she'd never again waste time waiting for what others had no intention of giving. It hurt to remember how pathetic she'd been back then, so sure that he wouldn't have abandoned her and desperate to hear from him, checking her phone for a message as soon as she woke up, leaping every time she received a new notification. Only none of them had been from him. She had only prolonged her own agony and wouldn't make the same mistake with Caleb. No, her eyes were wide open this time.

It would be a lie to say there wasn't a small part of her that was sad about that, for ideally, she would love for her child to know their father, but she needed to focus her emotion and energy on the more practical plans, such as finding somewhere to live and finding a way to stay in Kit's and Alexis's lives. Right now, she had little idea of how she'd manage either, and along with the prospect of single motherhood, she did feel somewhat daunted as she lay in bed unable to sleep, but Serena trusted she would figure it out. She had to. And given all the ways that life, and the people she'd been unfortunate enough to know, had taught her that the only person she could really rely on was herself, it was probably better that she was doing it alone anyway.

'Is that everything?' Caleb asked of his assistant, handing the relevant files back to her and arranging the papers that needed his signature.

'There's one more thing,' Nicole replied, pausing ever so slightly. 'An email has come through to the public account, but it's addressed personally to you. From a woman named Serena Addison.'

Serena. The mention of her name had Caleb's body stirring in ways that it hadn't in weeks. Not since the night he'd met her. Ever since that encounter he'd struggled to summon a shred of sexual interest for any of the women who had made themselves known to him, women of beauty and sophistication and experience, women with whom a night of debauched sex would be greatly enjoyed and wouldn't trouble his conscience. But now, that flash of her face in his mind, with that sexy tumble of red-gold hair and those bewitching amber eyes, promoted a landslide of torrid recollection—her tight hot heat and the ecstatic feeling in his blood as he'd thrust eagerly into her, the bite of her hands as she clung to him in delight, begging silently for more—and his body fired to life. Heat, rapid and relentless, swarmed in his blood and his groin hardened to an almost painful degree.

Whilst it was a relief to know that he was still capable of feeling desire, Caleb found it unbelievably frustrating that it was prompted by *her*. Because he didn't long for repeat encounters with women he'd already bedded, and it still burned that he had bedded her in the first place. It was an error he'd had no business making, and delving into why only reminded him how utterly he'd lost his head over her, and losing his control over a woman was not something he regarded with any pleasure at all. And whilst he had no problem still berating himself after eight long weeks, whatever he had felt for her that night should have dissipated entirely. Her name certainly shouldn't have the capability to charge his body with such a fierce, erotic longing that he was having to battle to shut it down. It shouldn't please him that she obviously hadn't forgotten him after all. And it certainly shouldn't be on the tip of his tongue to ask what she wanted, because it didn't matter. He wasn't going to see her again. Yet the question was pushing at his mind, testing his boundaries.

'You know how I feel about unsolicited communications from women,' he said, his jaw clenched with the effort required to force out the words. 'Delete it.'

Nicole hesitated again. 'I think you should read it.'

Without waiting for his agreement, she laid the tablet on the glass-topped desk before him, and unease leapt in the pit of his stomach. Nicole, who he appreciated so greatly because she followed his every instruction to the smallest requirement, would only insist if it was serious, if there was something in the correspondence that he *needed* to know.

There were very few things that Serena could have to impart that would directly affect him, and none of them were good.

The unease morphed into a tempest of foreboding that swirled ominously as he lowered his eyes to the device, absorbing the words of the brief message once. And then again.

Atop the desk his hand curled into a fist as his heart pounded. *Pregnant.*

She was claiming that she was pregnant with his child!

Emotion pulsed at the crown of his head—a frenzied, frantic feeling—and there was so much breath backing up in his lungs that his chest puffed outwards so hard that the buttons of his shirt strained.

'I take it that what she's saying is possible?' Nicole queried gently when he didn't speak.

'It's not impossible,' Caleb admitted with difficulty, his stomach turning over with the words. But exactly how *probable* was it, he questioned with the kind of cool and ruthless logic that reigned over all of his dealings.

He and Serena had only had sex once, and he had used protection. He always did, specifically to avoid a situation like this. So, the odds that she was actually pregnant, and if she was, that the child was his, were not favourable.

Suspicion buzzed loudly in his ears. Was she hoping to trap him into the type of relationship that he'd been explicit about not wanting? Had she researched him and realised the wonderful opportunity that he presented. He was socially astute enough to understand the powerful lure of his wealth and status. He knew others who'd been the target of similar abhorrent schemes. Serena had spoken about being boxed in, about her job not being her dream existence, he remembered with a burst of memory that was discomfortingly clear, so had she decided that he could be her ticket to a better life, a convenient escape from mundanity and responsibility?

Anger scorched its way along his veins, and yet part of him resisted the notion that the woman with alluringly amber eyes who had responded to him with such earnest eagerness could be capable of deceit.

And Caleb always heeded his instincts; they rarely steered him wrong. But he had already been wrong about who Serena was once, and this was not a matter that he could approach without question or caution. Not when there was such a high stake. *Fatherhood.*

Something he'd never sought. Something he wouldn't be any good at.

Something he didn't want to believe could be happening.

And he certainly wasn't about to allow himself to became ensnared in a ploy that was as old as time itself. He couldn't just take her word for it; he had to get to the truth of the matter himself, and if she was lying, well, he'd have no more trouble erasing her from his mind.

But if she is telling the truth? If she is pregnant with your child?

The questions were only a whisper in his head, but they were impossible to silence…

Serena was leaving work for the day when she heard her phone ringing and she dug into her pocket to snatch it up quickly in case it was either Kit or Alexis.

'Hello?' she asked, so eager to hear either of their voices that she failed to glance at the caller ID.

It had been ten days since she'd seen them, the longest they had ever gone without contact. The few video chats they had managed didn't count, as they'd been brief and conducted in whispers to ensure Marcia didn't overhear.

As Serena had feared, it hadn't taken long for her ever-watchful stepmother to realise Serena's stomach virus was in fact not a virus, and she had wasted no time in venting her disappointment and disapproval and banishing Serena from the house, much to the twins' dismay. She hadn't had any luck finding somewhere else to live that was close to the twins and within her budget, but fortunately, Evie had offered to let Serena stay with her. The separation from her siblings, however, was less easily fixed.

She was missing them and worrying about them desperately. Sensitive Kit had been distraught at the upheaval and the loss of Serena from the house, and even Alexis, who was normally the more placid and adaptable of the two, was struggling to accept the situation. And as much as Marcia doted on them, she was far too conservative to be able to offer much help with modern-day tween concerns. Serena was the one they turned to with those troubles, and it was killing her that she was shut out of being there should they need her, and that she was falling short of the promise she'd long ago made her to her mother to always remain close to them.

Each day that passed without that changing only deepened her feelings of failure and helplessness, but what made it even worse was that, buried beneath that anguish, was a buoyant relief that she was finally free from her stepmother's clutches. Free to do what she wanted, go wherever she pleased, wear what she liked. Serena couldn't enjoy it, not with so many uncertainties hovering over her and breeding anxiety in her heart, but just knowing that life was once more her own, and that most of what happened going forwards was in her sole and entire control, was like breathing fresh air after being stuck underground.

'Serena.'

She froze mid step. The voice belonged to neither Kit or Alexis, but it was still far more familiar than it should be and sent a shock wave straight to her heart. 'Caleb?' she gasped, when she finally found her voice.

'I'm in London.' Her grip on her phone tightened, because those words were even more unexpected than the velvet familiarity of his voice and sent panic wheeling across her chest. 'I want to meet up.'

'Why?'

'*Why*?' he repeated in an astounded pitch. 'Because we have something fairly important to discuss, don't you think?' *Did they?* Everything she had wanted to say to him, she had said in her email and couldn't imagine what would be weighing so heavily on his mind when she'd made it clear that she required nothing from him. Not his participation, his support, his money—not a single thing. Surely, that was the ideal outcome for him…so why on earth was he here? 'Are you free right now?'

Serena's heart thumped with annoyance. Did he really think that he could just show up and demand a piece of her time with no forewarning and that she would jump? 'No, I'm working late this evening,' she lied, feeling not even the teensiest bit bad about doing so. It wasn't as if she owed him anything. She'd done her duty by telling him about the baby and, if she did agree to sit down with him at some point, and that was a big *if*, then she wanted more preparation than a few seconds, wanted her thoughts to be ordered and eloquent and she was feeling neither of those things in that moment.

The sound of his voice had undone her, propelled her back to that night in Singapore, to all that she had felt that she didn't want to remember. How much worse would it be if she actually had to see him? How would she be able to meet those quicksilver eyes and not feel, not remember it all in exquisitely painful and hypnotising detail?

It had been hard enough squelching everything he'd awoken in her, forgetting the joy of their connection and how it felt to not be lonely. She didn't need that box opened.

'Is that so?' Caleb drawled. 'Because someone who looks exactly like you seems to be exiting your office building at this very second.'

Serena stiffened. *He was here, watching her?*

Her heart thudded again and frustration had her gritting her teeth together, not because she'd been caught out, but because he had obviously been testing her, and it was a test she had failed.

Casting her eyes left and right, it was then that she noticed the black Escalade, parked only a few feet away. Before she could say or think anything else, the door was opening and a long, strong body was emerging to stand on the pavement before her. He was dressed in a dark suit and coat, both of which screamed designer and only enhanced his towering six-foot-three, unrepentantly masculine appeal.

Through either the monstrous efforts of self-preservation or the passage of time, Serena wasn't sure which, the memory of what a breathtakingly formidable presence he was to behold had dimmed to something more palatable, but as he faced her down, there was no hiding from the truth of him. His full spectacular force filled her vision, and her heart thumped again. Harder.

'Hello, Serena.'

The face that regarded her was hard, and unnervingly cool eyes observed her with even more implacability. The strain on her senses intensified, and the sense of foreboding inched even higher up her spine, yet still she stood, devouring him with her eyes, wary, and yet also very, very *aware*.

Of how the coat hugged the width of his shoulders. How his eyes, even in evident displeasure, still seemed to glow. How he commanded the air surrounding him. And that was when she felt it, that slow-moving ripple across her skin, which made her tingle all the way down to her bones and which she wanted to quell at all costs.

'Why didn't you say from the outset that you were outside my office waiting for me?' she demanded, crossing her arms over her chest and staring at him with as much coolness as she could muster, which was exceedingly difficult when heat continued to rise in her like a lethal tide.

The brief movement of his sharp features offered no kind of answer. 'Why did you lie about working late?'

'Because I'm tired,' Serena shot back without taking a breath, her nerves rattling very close to the surface now. 'I've had a long day and an even longer week, and I really don't feel like having this conversation right now.'

'Well, now you have no choice in the matter.' He checked his watch. 'I reserved us a table at a place nearby. We should be going if we're to make it on time.'

Serena didn't move. 'I meant what I said, Caleb. I'm tired.'

'As am I,' he said, closing the short distance between them with two forceful, impatient strides. 'I've spent twenty hours flying halfway across the world, but the sooner we have this conversation the sooner we can both go home and get some rest.'

Stalking back to the car, Caleb held the door open, expectancy glowing in the steely eyes that glared over at her. Stubbornness kept Serena planted exactly where she was. She had never responded well to being told what to do and liked it even less since Marcia had thoroughly abused the power, and she resented the hell out of Caleb for airdropping into her day and issuing his arrogant commands. But now that he was here, unease would eat away at her until she knew exactly what he wanted, and she didn't need that extra strain, not when she was trying so hard to keep her stress levels low to avoid the same fate for the pregnancy as last time. Huffing out a sigh, she stepped forwards. 'I'll give you one hour of my time,' she said, sweeping by him without making any eye contact and with care not to touch him as she slid into the warm interior of the car. 'Not a minute more.'

Serena watched the waiter carefully set down their drinks on the polished table, her chest tightening with every extra second that he took. Not a word had passed between herself and Caleb on the short car ride. They seemed to have tacitly agreed not to speak of the matter at hand until they had reached their destination, but now the air between them was stretched so taut that every breath she took was tainted with the bitter taste of tension. It also didn't help that her body felt...*electrified*. As if every nerve and every sense had sprung into quivering life. Not with fear, but with something else...something she didn't want to name or think of or feel as acutely as she did. What she wanted was for this—whatever it was— to be over so she could get on with her evening. Her life.

'You seem nervous, Serena,' he commented as she clattered her spoon against her cup

Slowly, she lifted her eyes to look at him, feeling thrumming through her as their gazes clashed. 'Wasn't that the whole point of your ambush outside of my office? To catch me off guard and throw me off balance?'

Caleb was a man who liked to always have the upper hand. Even if Serena hadn't already deduced that from their brief interaction, one look at him, with his towering stance and determined jaw, would have confirmed it. The problem right now was that he didn't have control—after all, she was the one carrying his child and making decisions that could impact his life—but it was clear that he wanted the power back where he believed it rightfully belonged—in his hands. And that he would make whatever moves he could to get it back.

'I think *ambush* is a little extreme,' he responded levelly. 'I would have been in contact, but prior to setting off I wasn't one hundred percent sure of my plans. Once I was here, I thought it was more expedient to come to you straight away so we could talk about the situation.'

Something in her coiled as he referred to her pregnancy as a *situation,* but she was grateful for the anger as it singed away some of the nerves, infusing her instead with the strength required to force her way through this laborious conversation without giving away anything she didn't want to. Her power, for one.

That was something she was never surrendering again. Ever.

'So, talk.'

He fixed his grey gaze on her, as stormy as the skies beyond the window. 'You are pregnant?'

'I am.' His eyes seemed to drill deeper into her. 'If you were hoping to see some proof of that on my body, you're a few months early.'

He leaned forwards. 'I don't understand how it could have happened.'

'I would have thought you'd understand the basic facts of life.'

Annoyance flared in his slate gaze and Serena felt a small dart of childish pleasure that she was getting under his skin. 'What I mean is we only had sex once, Serena. *Once.* And I used protection. I always do.'

'Clearly it wasn't as effective as either of us would have liked,' she muttered, taking a small sip of her tea.

'You weren't taking a contraceptive pill?'

'No. I had no reason to be.'

A muscled flickered in his jaw. 'You seem very calm about all of this.'

'If my choice is between being calm or hysterical, I choose calm.' She hadn't been hysterical last time, but she hadn't been far from it. Being eighteen and pregnant, her emotions had been all over the place, and those feelings of fear and overwhelm had only spun more out of control when Lucas had deserted her. She carried a lot of guilt over that, certain that her fraught emotional state had contributed to her miscarriage, and she was determined that couldn't happen again. This time, she would keep herself in check, take care of herself. 'And it's not as though being worked up about it will change anything, is it? Nor would it do any good to me or the baby.'

It was impossible to miss the flare in his eyes at mention of the baby. 'So, you are planning to continue with the pregnancy then?'

'Yes. That's not up for discussion,' she added warningly, noting the spike of emotion in his expression. Was it panic? Frustration? Dread? It occurred to her then, with a rush of distress, that perhaps that was why he had made the long journey to London, to try and compel her to abort the pregnancy. The thought rattled her, and she settled an arm protectively across her stomach. 'So, if that is what you came all this way to talk about, you had a wasted journey.' She only just managed keep her voice civil.

'You think I would fly more than halfway around the world to pressure a woman into terminating a pregnancy?' he demanded, his horrified expression appearing to be genuine in its offence. 'That's the type of man you think I am?'

'How would I know?' Serena posited, refusing to feel quelled by his response. 'I don't know you, do I?'

She knew how his skin tasted on her tongue, she knew the strength contained in his chest and arms and how it felt to be locked against his body and trapped in his silvery gaze. They were things she hadn't been able to forget however hard she'd tried—things she wasn't sure she'd ever be able to forget—but that was physical. Irrelevant. Emotionally, she had no idea who Caleb Morgenthau was.

For a brief moment, Serena had thought she did. She'd thought that they understood one another in a way that had been rare and rich. As much as a she'd known nothing could really come of it, that moment of connection had been like finding a rare jewel, one that she could take out and admire on her hardest days, but then he had turned so cool and remote, so perturbed by her lack of sexual experience that everything that had come before had been proven false and it had hit her like a freezing wave that she really didn't know him at all. Just as she hadn't known Lucas. The resulting disillusionment had been even more chilling than the realization, and that had only made her want to flee even faster. She wouldn't be making the same mistake twice, presuming to know what kind of heart guided his intentions and motivations. She had to be guarded. There was no other choice.

'*Exactly*,' he exclaimed, seizing upon the word with a vehemence that warned his emotions were far closer to the surface and far more volatile than Serena had first reckoned. 'You don't know me.'

'But I do know what you told me that night in Singapore, which is that family and commitment hold no appeal for you.'

He had been upfront about that, and Serena hadn't expected it to suddenly change. That was why she had been so unprepared for the sight of him. If her actual boyfriend, someone who had professed to love her, had run away from her and their baby, why would Caleb, a man she'd spent only a single night with, go to the special length of crossing the globe to be involved? In a perfect world, maybe, but Serena knew the world wasn't perfect. It could be unfair and unkind.

Losing her mother so young had taught her that, and just when she'd been finding some kind of equilibrium, life had taken her father from her. Again, she'd picked herself up, found a way forwards, and when she'd thought happiness was in striking distance, that she could build a new life with Lucas and their baby and the twins and finally have a whole and happy family life again, cruelty had struck once more. So, she had to tailor her expectations to reality to keep from being broken all over again.

Looking him in the eyes, she took a steadying breath. 'Look, Caleb, the reason I told you about the pregnancy is because I believe you have a right to know, and so that if one day, twenty years from now, this child wants to find you, it won't be a complete shock. But that's the *only* reason. I wasn't trying to induce some reluctant involvement on your part when I know that's the last thing you want. I certainly wasn't expecting you to interrupt your life and fly all the way here…'

'I was coming to Europe anyway. I have business in the South of France,' he interrupted. 'I continue there tomorrow.'

She was just a pit stop, then. It was hard to decide whether to be relieved or insulted by that, but Serena settled on relieved, the admission making some kind of sense to her, given what she knew of him. He had ventured in her direction only because he was in the vicinity and he wanted to see how big of a problem she was to be solved, and that was something she could set his mind at ease on right away.

'My point is, I never had any expectation that your feelings would miraculously change overnight. I made this decision aware of that. So, this—' she gestured with a wave of her hand between them '—you being here, checking in, whatever it is you're doing, isn't necessary. At all.'

If anything, her words seemed to have caused even darker storm-clouds to gather in his eyes. 'On the contrary, *if* you are pregnant, and *if* I am the father, then I have certain responsibilities. Surely you would agree on that point?'

'*If,*' Serena scoffed, trying not to be offended and failing, because it was impossible to misunderstand the ugly intention behind his question. He was all but accusing her of being an opportunist, or even worse! 'You think I'm making this up?'

Briefly, the expression in his eyes seemed to shift, *soften,* and she thought he was going to reassure her that he did believe her, but in an instant, they'd regained their hard glitter. 'In the same way you don't know me, I don't know you well enough to make an assessment on what you would or wouldn't do.' Even as he said that, Serena knew that he had already made an assessment—and one that hurt. 'So, to start with, I'm here for my own confirmation that this pregnancy is real.'

As much as Serena would have liked him to take her word for it, she supposed it was a fair and pragmatic request and one she shouldn't judge him too harshly for. As a man of wealth and prominence, he had every reason to seek his own clarification. Not that she was sure why he wanted it when she didn't anticipate him doing much with it. He hadn't exactly refuted her suggestion that he didn't need to be involved, had he? Yes, he'd made mention of responsibilities, but what ones exactly? Nothing about him screamed hands-on parenting was anywhere in his future. His custom designer suit certainly wouldn't hold up well around the bodily functions of a baby. Serena could only surmise that he was thinking of financial responsibilities, offering a lump sum in lieu of anything else. She didn't have to wonder too hard about why that option would appeal to him.

'OK. I can arrange to have a blood test and have you copied in on the results. I'll call my doctor, but it may take a few days to get an appointment.'

'I have a doctor who has agreed to fit us in and do the test this evening,' Caleb announced.

'Of course you do.'

'At my request, and with your consent, she will also perform a DNA test.'

Serena tensed, a fear-poisoned arrow shooting to her heart. She had heard about amniocentesis, the needle and possible side effects, and with panicked breath building in her chest, she started to shake her head. She was absolutely not risking her pregnancy just so he could have...

'There's no need to look alarmed,' Caleb said, almost too kindly. 'I've been assured its non-invasive and perfectly safe. Blood is taken from both of us and provided you are over eight weeks pregnant, which if I am the father, you should be, fetal blood should be present with yours and be a match for mine.'

Although he hadn't moved an inch, his eyes seemed to regard her with even more probing intensity, as though trying to discern her every flicker of answering emotion. As the threatened beats of her heart began to subside, Serena nodded slowly. 'Alright.'

A small furrow cut into the space between his dark brows, as though he hadn't expected such easy agreement and Serena quickly realised that he had been watching—hoping for?— the opposite reaction.

'And when these tests prove that I am pregnant with your child, what then?' she asked, because it was clear that he preferred the idea that this was some crazy scheme rather than that she was actually carrying his child, and that he would in all likelihood walk away, even once he had his confirmation.

'Let's just take this one step at a time, OK, Serena,' he said, through lips suddenly tight with tension.

His unwillingness to commit to anything disappointed her, even though it was what she'd known would happen. 'Shall we get going then?' she said, getting to her feet, eager to move on.

The sooner they got this over with, the sooner he could go on his merry way and leave her to carry on picking up the pieces of her life and putting them back together to create a new and hopefully far happier one.

CHAPTER FOUR

'WE SHOULD ARRIVE at the airfield in about forty minutes, sir.'

'Good. Thank you.' Caleb nodded his gratitude to his driver as he settled himself into the luxurious interior of the car, his departure from London not coming a moment too soon. He couldn't wait to put this whole sordid pregnancy ordeal behind him and never think of it again.

Never think of Serena Addison again either.

And how are you going to do that? You've been trying to put her from your mind for weeks without any success, and seeing her again in the flesh certainly hasn't helped!

Tenison buzzed through Caleb's veins, too much truth within that burst of thought for him to dismiss it as easily as he wanted to. Seeing Serena again yesterday had stirred a greater reaction than he had been prepared for, igniting a fire in his blood that had continued to smoulder long after they had parted ways...

Watching from the darkened window of the car, his intent had been to observe her unvarnished reaction to his presence, but the moment she had exited her office building, unmissable with her striking long legs and slim body and that sexy tumble of strawberry hair, he hadn't wanted to do anything except stare. Devour the sight of her because she was even more beautiful than he had remembered. Heat had kindled low in his stomach, and the tug of awareness deep in his groin had been fierce, so potent that the anger churning through him ever since reading that damned email and burning so hotly he hadn't slept at all on the journey to London, had been stilled into near submission.

The wave of desire had been so strong that for a moment he had forgotten—*actually forgotten*—his reason for being there as his mind flooded with heated imaginings of those long legs locked tightly around his waist and his face buried in the sweet-smelling, and even sweeter-tasting, hollow of her neck as he drove himself deep into her body. Wrenching himself from the sensual daydream had taken supreme effort, and even then, tendrils of smoky heat continued to curl through his bloodstream, threatening to pull him back under should he lose control for even the barest of seconds. The frustration he'd felt with himself for that lapse, and the continuing weakness where she was concerned, had only made him even more unyielding when they had finally stood face-to-face. Because as much of a nuisance as his undying desire for her was, it was an even greater aggravation hat he was burning up inside for someone who could be trying to dupe him.

However, the longer he'd spent with her, the harder it had been to keep his suspicions burning. Nothing about her seemed deceitful, and she had agreed easily to all that he'd asked, as though she truly had nothing to hide.

The conundrum of it had kept him awake into the early hours, uncomfortable with his assumptions about her. Yet he just couldn't accept the other option—that she was being honest and he was going to be a father.

A notification alert on his phone drew his attention, and withdrawing it from his inner pocket, Caleb was happy to see it was the results of the pregnancy and DNA test. Finally, the matter could be put to bed for good, and before he reached the South of France so he would be able to proceed with the urgent matters on the new Saint-Tropez beach club without any distractions. Except...

His heart thumped uncomfortably and the air in his chest grew thin. Tight.

Serena *was* pregnant.

And the test confirmed that he was the father.

Caleb shook his head. It was impossible. It couldn't be. It couldn't...and yet it was, he accepted, glancing again at the test results, which he had been assured were 97 percent accurate.

He was going to be a father. There was shock and disbelief spreading at an alarming speed across his chest, but amongst that turbulence there was also an unassailable clarity and, although he was suddenly in a situation he'd never wanted to find himself in, Caleb knew exactly what he had to do.

'Turn the car around.'

The driver startled, eyes flicking to the rearview mirror. 'Sir? I thought you had a flight you needed to...'

'What I need is to go back into the city,' Caleb snapped impatiently. 'Turn the car around now!'

The queue of traffic heading into the capital was far greater than the line heading out, so the car crawled for long stretches of time, but Caleb barely noticed, too lost in his own web of thoughts.

There were many reasons why he'd never entertained the notion of fatherhood. He was selfish, for starters. He worked ridiculously long hours and rarely spent more than a year in one city before moving on again. He had no stellar example to emulate. His father had often worked so late into the night that he'd slept at his office and left the rearing of his son to a rotation of highly qualified nannies. And having spent the majority of his life studiously avoiding getting close to anyone and feeling anything, to prevent the mess of emotion and pain that had stained his childhood, it was now less of a habit and more of an ingrained way of being that Caleb wasn't sure could be changed. Or that he particularly wanted to change.

However, all of those reasons paled in comparison to the main motive, the one that was never far from his mind, that whispered its fearful prophecy in his ear whenever his father instigated another of his imploring conversations about continuing the family line and securing their future legacy—the chilling knowledge that, should he let someone into his life, someone who could grow to care about him, he would only end up hurting them.

Just as he had hurt Charlotte.

He may not intend to, but it was inevitable that he would. Hurting Charlotte was the last thing he'd wanted, but it had happened. Just by being himself.

You ruined her. Our beautiful daughter and you ruined her. She loved you and you didn't deserve it.

Caleb's heart never failed to race whenever he recalled

those words that Charlotte's parents had hurled at him in the corridor of the hospital when he'd attempted to visit, armed with flowers and an apology, the apology he should have offered her hours earlier, the apology that could have prevented the horrible, tragic mess that had unfolded. Only he hadn't been able to get anywhere near Charlotte to tell her how sorry he was or how awful he felt. Faced with her family's anger and his own suffocating sense of responsibility, he'd fled, but he'd never been able to erase the image of their devastated faces, ravaged by rage and pain…so much pain for their beloved daughter and her lost future—the future that, before him, had been so bright and full of opportunity.

Charlotte had been in Melbourne for a prestigious summer internship when they'd met. Unacquainted with the city or its social elite, she'd had no knowledge of his reputation for cycling through women, and he hadn't taken the time to tell her, because he didn't explain himself to anyone. He was a Morgenthau and he did whatever he wanted, whenever he wanted, with whomever he wanted. It had never crossed his mind that she would fall in love with him because love was the last thing on his agenda. Caleb had no intention of feeling that, not for her, not for anyone, not after the emotional carnage of his childhood. When Charlotte had finally realised that, she'd been devastated.

She had raged at him. Sobbed and shouted and eventually stormed from the club, and in her tearful, broken-hearted state had rammed her car straight into a wall, shattering her body the way Caleb had shattered her heart.

It wasn't until late the next day that Caleb learned what had happened, but once he did, he'd been racked with guilt. Who could doubt that it was his fault when it was his cruelty that had caused the accident? Had Charlotte not been in such an anguished state, she would never have lost control of the vehicle, wouldn't have gotten in the car at all. And he'd seen how distressed she was. Why hadn't he gone after her, stopped her? The heavy pounding of guilt had consumed him, and the angry reaction of her parents had confirmed the fault he bore.

And Caleb had known then, with a certainty as clear as water, that he couldn't allow anyone remotely close to him again. Because they would only end up hurting too, and he couldn't bear to inflict that magnitude of pain of another unsuspecting, innocent heart.

And it would happen again. He knew that. Because Charlotte wasn't the first person to be devastated by him. Years earlier, Caleb had destroyed his father when he'd driven away his mother, leaving Adlai Morgenthau a desolate, grief-stricken shell of himself. But after Charlotte, he was determined there would be no others.

He'd stuck to that resolve ever since, careful in ways he'd never been before about the type of women he spent his nights with, strict about limiting their involvement to a single encounter, a period of time too brief for any feelings, for *anything real*, to develop. The only misstep he'd ever made was with Serena…a misstep that still sent chills down his spine because with her inexperience and emotionality, there were so many ways he could have hurt her.

And now that she was carrying his child, there were many more.

Despite his knee-jerk reaction to return to the capital, instinct was once again urging him that the best thing he could do for Serena and for the child was to leave them alone. Generously provide, of course, but from afar, where they would be spared the harm that he would eventually cause and he could spare himself the burden of having to live with disappointing them.

But how could he just turn away from his child, his own flesh and blood, the way he turned away from everyone else?

Especially when he knew what it was to grow up with only one parent. He knew the persistent ache of abandonment, the questions that filled that yawning empty space—questions destined never to be answered. He knew it was a void that could be painted over and ignored, but still, somehow, remained. Could he really condemn his son or daughter to that fate?

There were other considerations charging through his mind too. Practical ones. This child would be the sole heir to the Morgenthau name and empire. Whilst he had been unwilling to bring an innocent child into the world just to satisfy his father's wish to safeguard the future, now there was a child, so it was a different consideration altogether. It wasn't about creating a life. That had already happened; now it had to be about protecting them as best he could, ensuring they received all the privilege and security their blood entitled them to. He was the only one with the power to guarantee that. And he had to.

There was no certainty of what kind of father he would be, so he had to give his child every protection possible.

From deep within his chest his heart kicked, his stomach twisting as he approached an uneasy decision. Instinct might still be screaming at him the same old message, that the best thing he could do was stay far away from both Serena and the baby, but he could feel the tug of other instincts now too, paternal ones, and they would countenance nothing of the sort.

CHAPTER FIVE

SHOCK PINNED SERENA to the spot as she pulled open the front door and found herself staring into a set of smoky grey eyes. 'Caleb,' she breathed, her heart quickening as he filled the doorway. In another of his bespoke suits, this one a perfect match for the shade of his eyes, with a crisp white shirt beneath, he was a devastating sight. 'What are you doing here?'

'I got the test results back a short while ago,' he answered, his gaze heavy. 'The DNA is a match. You're carrying my child.'

One hand clung to the door for support because her knees had turned to water, but Serena managed to pull herself up taller and meet his eyes fearlessly, even as flickers of apprehension licked at the sides of her stomach. Wasn't he supposed to be on his way to the South of France? 'You came here to tell me something I already know?'

'No. I'm here to discuss our next steps. Preferably not on the doorstep.' He scowled, brushing past her, and Serena didn't even try to stop him, stumbling as she was over his use of the word *our*—as though this was a situation they were in together. Which, yes, biologically they were. But in every other way, they absolutely weren't.

'What exactly do you mean *our* next steps?' Serena asked urgently, trailing him into the living space and scanning his face for some clue that would help her ward off her rapidly descending sense of alarm—but he was as inscrutable as ever. 'Because I told you yesterday that I'm perfectly happy to raise this child alone…' she reminded him, striving to keep her voice steady even though she felt as if she was suddenly hovering over a minefield and, with any step, there would be an explosion.

'And I'm telling you today that whatever you thought yesterday is not acceptable to me.' His eyes glowed down at her in a way that made her far too aware of the unfettered leaping of her heart and pulse. 'There is no world in which any child of mine will grow up without my name, or without me being in their life. So, you and I are going to get married.'

The word detonated in Serena's ears and it was a moment before the disorientation cleared enough for her to form words. 'Married?' she repeated, hoping he would tell her that she had misheard him, but that hope sank as he made a single, controlled gesture of his dark head. She shook her head, backing away from him and from the treacherous frissons that were firing through her at the thought. 'I don't…no. You and I are not going to get married, Caleb. That's insane.'

'Actually, it's highly pragmatic,' he countered emotionlessly. 'You're pregnant with my child—it's the logical next step. The *only* next step.'

'No. No, it's not. Because this is the twenty-first century. A pregnancy no longer mandates a ring.'

In some situations, perhaps, but definitely not theirs. They didn't know the first thing about one another. *That's not entirely true though, is it?* a voice in her head asked, stirring recollections of the night in Singapore, spine-tingling memories of how they had connected so quickly, so easily. Except they hadn't, she argued back. She only *thought* they had connected, wanting to believe it was more than it had been and that was a folly she had no excuse for. She should have learned from her experience with Lucas, because she'd done the same thing with him. Believing that they shared a special connection and that he would always be there for her. She didn't want to be that same stupid girl, making the same stupid mistakes, as she tried—hopelessly—to recreate the life and family she'd loved and lost. She wouldn't be!

Because that life that she'd known was gone—and trying to bring it back would only cause more heartbreak, which wasn't a risk she was willing to take.

'The baby can have your name without us being married, if that's so important to you. And you can be involved too. I'm sure we can figure something out,' she said, trying to keep hold of the control over her life that she'd only just regained. But she didn't quite manage to hide the edge of scepticism from her rush of words, because she wasn't sure she trusted that Caleb's commitment to being involved was quite as robust as he made out. Not when a day ago, hell, probably even an hour ago, he hadn't even been willing to accept his responsibility in the pregnancy. Not when he had stated clearly and with certainty that he didn't want any commitment in his life, and a child was the greatest commitment of all. A lifelong relationship. Lucas hadn't wanted that. So why would he?

'Serena...' Her name emerged from his full lips as part reasoning and part censure. 'Be reasonable.'

Her mouth almost hit the floor. How could he say that to *her* when he was the one suggesting something as absurd as marriage? 'You don't even want to be a father, Caleb. You don't want to get married.'

'True, on both counts,' he agreed calmly, moving in place and taking over even more of the damnably small living space with his dark, sex-edged, oozing masculinity. There wasn't anywhere that Serena could look and not feel him in her gaze, nowhere to stand where she could be unaffected by the power that vibrated off him. 'But things have changed. Now I am going to be a father and that necessitates other changes and compromises. Especially if my child is to inherit all that is rightfully theirs.' Serena must have looked as nonplussed as she felt, because he sighed. 'The child you're carrying is the sole heir to my billion-dollar company, and I will not have them denied any of that because they were born illegitimate.'

'So, you only want to get married so they can inherit and run your company in twenty-five years?' she demanded, thinking that was hardly a sufficient reason.

'That's not the only reason, no,' he responded, obviously reading her lack of enthusiasm. 'But it is a pressing one. They are entitled to it, Serena. All of it. It's their birthright.'

That made her mind spin because it wasn't an aspect she had considered, or even realised was at stake, and that made her aware of just how out of her depth she was with Caleb. 'No. I won't do it. I can't. I'm not marrying you.'

His expression hardened with displeasure, but also with determination. 'Give me one good reason why not.'

'I'll give you two. I don't love you and I don't trust you.'

He dismissed her feelings with a motion of his hand. 'That's of no consequence. I don't require either your love or your trust, or for us to have any substantial relationship of any kind. All I require is your hand in marriage for all the world to see.'

This time her mouth did fall open at the dearth of emotion in his words, so at odds with the determination smouldering in his eyes. So, he was proposing a marriage in name only, with no feeling, no friendship even, between them? How could he so blithely give his life away to someone he didn't at least care for in some small way? And how dare he expect her to?

'There's no need to look so indignant. What I'm suggesting may not be to your personal taste, but it makes perfect sense.'

How did it? Marriage wasn't a solution to a problem. It was a solemn vow between two people who adored one another, just as her parents had. Having watched their marriage, Serena had always believed that it should only be considered when a deep and abiding love and trust were present. And as she'd said, she didn't love or trust Caleb. He was so high-handed that he'd be the last man she'd want to marry. He'd been there less than a minute and was already trying to take over her life, and as for trusting anyone ever again...after Lucas had stomped all over her heart in his haste to desert her, that was definitely unlikely to happen. Why would she sign up for more heartbreak?

'Not to me it doesn't,' she riposted.

In surviving all that she had, Serena had learned the valuable lesson that the one and only person she could, and should, truly rely on was herself. It was safer and smarter that way.

'That's because you're thinking with your heart, and not your head,' he said with mild condemnation, his eyes sweeping over her and rousing tingles that she fought not to feel.

He was silent a moment, as though expecting her to change her mind, and when she didn't, his sensual lips firmed into a flat line of displeasure, a storm whipping to life in his gaze that had pulses of frenetic nervous energy zinging from one side of her body to the other. But crossing her arms over her chest, partly to hide the merciless rhythm of her heart that hadn't once ceased in his presence, Serena held her ground.

Was he really endowed with such arrogance that he'd expected she would jump at the chance to be his wife? Or was he just too used to everyone he surrounded himself with falling in line with his wishes that he'd forgotten that people had minds of their own? Both, she decided, as she watched his jaw sharpen with a fresh burst of resolve.

He moved towards her, a hard smile smoothing over his wicked mouth, a mouth she remembered all too well. How it moved. Tasted. How it had claimed her moans again and again and again. She fought to stay in the moment and not drift back to that night spent in his arms, but that had been a difficult enough task when he hadn't been in London. Now that he was here, and so tantalisingly close, it was all too easy to sink into the memories, forget how he had hurt and humiliated her and remember only the exquisite bliss he had delivered...

'Just consider for a moment the life I can provide for you. The security and comfort,' he added, making a point of looking around the room. 'Far more than you'll know here. You have to admit it's a little cramped—what will it be like when you add a baby to it?'

His line of questioning cut too close to her own fears and concerns for her not to react. 'I'm only staying here temporarily—until I find someplace of my own.'

It was only as she watched his quick mind seize upon that information that she realised her error in snapping back.

'Why only temporarily? What happened to where you were living previously?'

'I... I had to move out,' she explained falteringly, loath to say any more than that because she knew that the truth would only weight the case in his favour.

'Because...?'

'My stepmother doesn't approve of the pregnancy,' she said when the silence became unbearable. 'Or how I came to be pregnant.'

His eyes narrowed, reading between the lines of what she'd said. 'She threw you out?'

Serena could only manage a small nod of her head, the pain of it still raw, the way she had failed her siblings still a barbed lump rolling around her chest, as well as her failure to find a way to fix it.

'Your father didn't have anything to say about that?'

'My father passed away six years ago,' she shared, her heart sore.

Caleb's expression changed; so too did his body, angling more fully in her direction. In an instant, she was under the intense spotlight of his gaze, and that made her feel unaccountably breathless. Trapped. Especially as his expression was suddenly so full of sympathy. 'Serena, I'm so sorry. That must have been—must still be— awful for you.'

'It was a long time ago. It's fine.'

Wrenching her gaze away, she tried to think about something else, *anything else*, because that show of heartfelt sympathy was pushing on something that she didn't want to be touched. Couldn't afford to be touched. Because she needed to remain strong, just as she'd always had to be, and if she were to dwell on how much she longed for her parents right now, or how alone she felt in the dark of night and how truly, deeply worried she was for the future, for Kit and Alexis, for her baby, she might just fall apart and she couldn't do that.

And why was it sympathy from this man, of all men, that was threatening to undo her? Threatening to unleash a torrent of emotion that would drown her, when for years she had mastered the art of squashing and compressing and storing it neatly away.

'It's not. Losing both parents at such a young age isn't something anyone should have to live through.' There was such sincerity in his voice that her fight only grew harder. 'And not having family support must be difficult. I know I'm not offering anything traditional, but I can provide plenty more. A home. Security. Support. Any-thing—*everything*—you could want. And our child will grow up with both of their parents in their life.' He lev-elled her with eyes that suddenly seemed to be made of steel. 'Which is as it should be, Serena. You know that. It matters to you that our baby grows up knowing who their father is, or you wouldn't have told me about the pregnancy at all.'

She cursed his logic. And when had he moved so close to her? His sudden nearness sparked an attraction that flared too hot and fast for her to have any hope of resist-ing. Or, much to her annoyance, concealing. She could feel his heat and power and strength winding their way around her like the threads of a spell, rendering her im-mobile. She could only stare up at him, saying nothing but feeling everything. If Caleb saw or felt those shim-mers of reaction streaking through her, he didn't show it.

'I'll give you some time to think it over. I'm sure that with a little consideration, you'll see it's the right thing to do. I'll see myself out.'

His eyes flashed down at her a final time before he turned away, stalking to the door, which he closed softly behind him. Only then did Serena realise how badly she was shaking, reeling from both his proposal and his presence.

The last thing she'd expected was for him to show up. She thought he'd be so eager to get to the South of France that he'd sprout wings and fly there himself, never to be heard from again. Just like Lucas. A brief pain pulsed in her heart as she remembered the agonising moment she realised he'd gone. And after that hurt had come the bruising disappointment. In him, but mostly in herself. For believing in Lucas so ardently that she'd ignored the warning signs that he wasn't who she wanted him to be and dismissed words of caution from others, including her stepmother, that he wasn't the right guy for her.

But she had been so in need of someone in her life. Someone to love her and hold her and fill that enormous empty space the loss of her parents had left. At least when she'd lost her mum, she'd still had her father. But when he died, there was no one. It was that aloneness that had been the hardest and scariest thing to deal with, and when, after only a matter of months, Marcia had started changing the house to suit her tastes, it had felt as if there was nothing left of the life she'd once known. Outside of her brother and sister, the only solace she'd been able to find was her friends, in the noise and laughter and fun that surrounded her when she was with them, drowning out the reality that she was suddenly an orphan. It was at that time that she'd met Lucas and he'd made her feel so much good that the bad had been pushed away.

But then he'd disappeared, forcing Serena to navigate another loss, followed quickly by the hardest one of all—her baby. The loss, which in her heart, she'd never stopped blaming herself for, and Serena didn't want to make any more mistakes—*couldn't*—and the only way she knew to do that was to stay separate, rely only on herself.

She'd been doing it so long already that it didn't faze her—much. Financially it would be challenging, but emotionally it would be far safer. Not being tempted to open herself up, not getting attached to someone only to then lose them and have the bottom drop out of her world again.

But is that the best thing for your baby?

Caleb was offering support and security, a life where their child would want for nothing. A life with two parents, and she knew how precious a gift that was. She wanted that for her child. And as much as she feared she had messed up once again, becoming entangled with someone as charming and careless as Lucas had been, Caleb had shown up. And he was determined to be involved. That made him different.

Serena paced to the opposite end of the room. Had Caleb been right? Had she reacted with her heart, been led by her fears?

But how could she not be afraid?

Life had slapped her in the face time after time. Every time she thought she'd found some stable ground, it had shifted under her. She'd lost almost everyone she'd ever loved, except the twins, but even they were lost to her now too—unless marrying Caleb could solve that also?

But if she agreed—and it all somehow went wrong? And how would she manage her strange feelings for him? How would she manage *him*? He was impossible and arrogant and high-handed, waltzing in as he had and expecting her to go along with his plan just because he'd decided it was for the best.

She'd only just gotten her life back. The thought of surrendering it again was hideous, and she really didn't want to. But if it was in the best interests of her baby, and Kit and Alexis, then could she really say no…?

Caleb would have preferred if Serena had agreed to his proposal straight away, but after his many years in business, he was used to dealing with difficult parties. He knew how impactful walking away from a negotiation could be, how it nearly always spurred the other side into a quick agreement to his terms, so as he made the journey to Serena's flat the next day, he was sure that after a night to consider her options, she'd be eager to accept his proposal. Almost sure, anyway. After witnessing her stubborn resistance yesterday, he'd learned there was nothing predictable about Serena. Any other woman would have leapt at the opportunity to marry him, especially one in her predicament.

An orphan. Banished from her home. No family support. It was hard to comprehend how much she had been through. It had hurt him to hear it, and he'd been overcome by a surge of protective instincts he hadn't known he possessed, wanting to provide the security and support that she'd been denied and to make everything bad in her life better, which was crazy, because when had he ever made anything better for anyone?

But he knew that their marrying would benefit Serena greatly, even if she was unwilling to see it. For one thing, she'd have a home that she couldn't be evicted from, and one with more square footage then a shoebox. She'd also have financial security for the rest of her life, but more importantly than all of that, she wouldn't have to raise their child on her own. She'd known enough struggles in her life already; he didn't want her to have to navigate parenthood alone too.

As he prepared to press again for her hand in marriage, those emotional considerations were as strong in his mind as the practical ones. No longer was he only thinking of pleasing his father with the continuation of the family line, or of guaranteeing his child's lifelong financial security, but of ensuring a better future for Serena too, free from any further angst. Caleb wasn't sure how he felt about that.

He reassured himself that it was for the good of their child as much as anything. A contented mother would be a better mother, and he wanted his child to have their mother in their life. To never know the bitter pain that had lived in him.

That was the most emotion he was willing to acknowledge because the last thing he wanted was for emotions to be part of the equation. And they weren't. He'd proposed marriage because he'd known instinctively it was what the situation demanded, *not* because of any desire to rescue her, or because knowing for certain that his child grew in her stomach had unleashed a fierce urge to claim her as his.

He didn't like the thought of marrying any more than he had before. His stomach writhed with unease at bringing Serena into his orbit, where hurt was not just a possibility, but a reality, especially after everything she'd already been through. Paradoxically, that was the best way for him to protect her and their unborn child. That was the reason—the only reason—he felt such desperation for her to agree to be his wife.

And he had considered the situation at length, with his customary focus and attention to detail, figuring out how it would work, how he would paint clear and thick boundaries between them. Even once she was his wife, he would hold Serena at arm's length the same way he did everyone. They would only interact wherever and whenever was necessary, and if it granted his child the emotional security that he had been denied, then that was what mattered most. The greatest thing he wished was for them to be whole and happy and loved and to know they were wanted. All of the things that he himself had yearned to know but never been sure of.

It was why he had awoken that morning even more aware of the importance of Serena agreeing to the marriage, and even more resolved to do whatever it took to ensure that outcome. It was with that determination powering his body that he alighted from the car and strode up the path to Serena's flat, his movement faltering as he saw the front door was ajar and he detected raised voices from within. His first and only thought was of Serena's safety, and without hesitating, he shouldered his way inside, every inch of his body primed to intervene in whatever was happening, before he slowed to listen to the heated argument in progress.

'They are my brother and sister. You have no right to keep us apart. They *need* me,' Serena cried. 'They've already lost their mother and father, the last thing they need is to lose me too. You have no idea what kind of negative impact this could have on them.'

'I don't see any negative effects of them being spared your vile influence,' hissed a cold female voice in response. 'Really, what kind of example are you, Serena? As if being pregnant out of wedlock *again* isn't bad enough, but to be pregnant from a fumble with someone you barely knew... It's shameful. It is definitely not the example I want Kit or Alexis to be exposed to, and it's not something I want to be associated with either. You knew the rules, Serena. And you chose to break them. You brought this on yourself. I wish I could say that surprises me, but you've always been headed for this kind of disgraceful, scandalous existence, and I will not let you drag Kit and Alexis down with you. I tried my best to steer you towards a better path, but...'

'Nothing you ever did was to try and help me,' Serena fired back, just as Caleb, having heard enough to understand exactly what was going on, stepped into the room, his protective instincts firing even harder. His sudden presence disturbed the taut, hostile air, and both women turned abruptly to look at him.

'Caleb...' Serena paled, blinking rapidly. 'Now isn't really a good time,' she pleaded, the emotional tremble wracking her voice causing even more unfamiliar feeling to strain within him. Not just to protect, but to comfort. To reassure her that she hadn't done anything wrong.

'I can see that.' He stepped to Serena's side, casting his eyes across her face quickly and reading the full depth of her distress. Something sharp seared across his chest as he did, the instinct to raise his hand to her cheek and stroke away all the pain rising within him. He resisted, *obviously*, swivelling his eyes to fix his attention on the other woman instead. 'You must be Serena's stepmother.'

'Marcia Addison,' she replied imperiously, and with

more courtesy that he knew he would have received had she not immediately been struck by his aura of power and wealth. She had been absorbing every detail of his person since he'd stepped into the room. He hadn't missed her eyes dusting over him, noting his custom-made suit, Italian handcrafted shoes and limited edition watch.

'It's lovely to meet you at last.' Supressing the anger still bubbling over the cruelty she had shown Serena, he sent her his most charming smile. 'I'm Caleb Morgenthau. Serena's fiancé.'

Her eyes widened, her eyebrows flying up into her hairline. 'Her... I'm sorry...her *fiancé*?'

'Yes,' he confirmed silkily, slipping his arm around Serena's waist to draw her tightly into his side. Serena tensed, but his secure grip neutralised her attempts to wriggle away, and the pleasure of how snugly she fitted against him infiltrated his mind and body with far too many sparks. Unbidden, memories of their night together flooded his brain—heated flashes of their seeking, open-mouthed kisses, their bodies kneading hungrily together, her flesh welcoming him—and an inferno of heat exploded in his core, but he clung to his focus. 'Please accept my apology for you only just this moment finding out, but I insisted on Serena and I sharing the news together in person, and business kept me from London until yesterday. That may, however, have been a mistake as it seems our happy news has caused some friction within your family.' He made sure to meet the woman's eyes, summoning all of his commanding power into his gaze. 'I'm sure it's nothing more than a misunderstanding, as surely you, and anyone else who cares to look, can see there's no scandal here. Just a young couple who've fallen in love in a whirlwind relationship and are starting their life together.' He gazed down at Serena the way he imagined a besotted man might, and it was far easier than he'd thought as his eyes indulged in her bright amber gaze and full, inviting mouth and a smile drew naturally across his lips. *Mine*, he thought, shocked by the possessive force of the thought. 'There's certainly no reason for anyone to have questions over Serena's propriety. And whilst I completely understand and respect your desire to protect your children from harmful influences, there are none here. Unless you consider joy and happiness to be harmful.'

'Well…of course not…' Marcia replied falteringly.

'Excellent, so there's no reason for there to be any further talk of Serena being a bad influence, and definitely no reason for three siblings who love and rely on each other very much to be kept apart any longer. Is there?' he demanded, daring her from behind his charm to defy him.

Her mouth thinned, tightened. 'If you are in fact getting married and starting a respectable family…then, no,' she agreed, reluctance underwriting her every word. 'There is no problem.'

'Perfect.' Caleb beamed, enjoying watching her almost choke on the words and catching a hint of a smile on Serena's lips too. 'Now, we would love to share this news with Kit and Alexis ourselves, so how about we arrange a visit for once they've finished school this afternoon? And as for the wedding,' Caleb continued, not offering her any chance to respond, 'it's planned for this weekend, in the South of France. It's set to be an extraordinary day, but please don't worry about the arrangements, I will take care of everything.'

'I look forward to it,' murmured Marcia, her skin losing colour rapidly. 'Now I had best be going.'

'I'll walk you out,' Caleb offered, gesturing for Marcia to precede him out into the hallway. 'I'd like to think I can rely on you to quash any further talk of scandal, Mrs Addison? I would hate for my fiancée's reputation to be impugned for no reason, and should I find out that people were talking of her in such a way, I would have to take quite drastic steps in response. That is a husband's prerogative, after all, to protect his wife from anyone who means her harm. *Anyone* at all,' he added, firing a pointed look that there was no chance of her misunderstanding

'I'm sure that won't be necessary,' she demurred.

'I hope not,' he said, seeing her into the street and smiling as she walked away, deflated and defeated, because victory was such a sweet taste, and a double victory…well, that was double the sweetness.

'What the hell was that?' Serena demanded, rounding on Caleb with temper blistering in her eyes as soon as he walked back through the door.

From his superior height, Caleb regarded her calmly, almost smugly, from eyes that blazed victorious. 'I think that the words you're looking for are *thank you*.'

'Thank you?' Serena parroted on a giant breath of disbelief. 'Thank you? You actually expect me to be grateful for the way you just railroaded me into a marriage that I hadn't agreed to.'

'I think you should be grateful that I just put your step-mother back in her box and enabled you to keep having a relationship with your siblings and to see them as soon as this afternoon.'

That took the wind right out of Serena's words because he had done exactly that and it was no small feat, mastering her stepmother in the way that he had. It wasn't something she'd ever been able to manage. Serena had never seen Marcia back down so quickly or be at such a loss for words, but she'd been no match for Caleb's lethal charm offensive. Watching it unfold had rendered her speechless and weak-kneed at his show of power. However, the fire raging in her chest was less easy to dampen because of *how* he had done it.

'By telling her that we're getting married. And this weekend!'

Caleb tipped his dark head ever so slightly, the steel in his eyes softening to silver. 'I'm afraid I saw no other way around it. You heard her, Serena. There was no way she was going to let you back into your siblings' lives, not whilst you were, at least in her eyes, disgraced.'

Arms crossed tightly across her chest, she glared back at him. 'Do not pretend that you did that to help me. You are not some knight in shining armour who just slew a dragon and rescued me from a tower.' Although there was some part of her that did feel rescued, and she hated that. Because she couldn't even start to believe he was someone she could rely on in that way. In any way. 'You saw an opportunity to get exactly what you wanted, and you seized upon it.'

'Perhaps I did. But I never claimed to be someone who wouldn't do whatever I have to, to get what I want, did I?' Shivers ran over her because he was so unapologetically arrogant, and it was dazzling. 'And it doesn't mean I didn't want to help you and your siblings. And why didn't *you* tell me that in addition to kicking you out, she was stopping you from seeing your brother and sister?' he asked, watching her from his gleaming gaze. 'How can she even get away with that?'

'Because she adopted them when they were little, right after she married my dad, so she has final say on everything. And I didn't say anything because it has nothing to do with you.'

She hated that she sounded like a petulant teenager, but the way he had crashed into her life and thrown out commands and now backed her in a corner from which she had no escape had sent her spinning back to all those other times where she'd felt utterly, horribly powerless, as if every drop of power she possessed was slipping from her grasp, and the harder she tried to catch and hold on to it, the more she lost. And now it was happening all over again. And it was worse, because as much as she wanted to loathe Caleb entirely—she didn't. Couldn't.

Because he had helped her. Without any hesitation. It had been so long since she'd had anyone on her side, anyone to fight for her when she felt weak. Her father had almost always taken her side in her scrapes with Marcia. With hindsight she could see how that had aggravated their tenuous relationship, their closeness only making Marcia harden towards her, but in spite of her stepmother's coolness, she'd known such safety, knowing her father was there to catch her if she stumbled or fell. But then, in a blink, he'd been gone and she'd been so alone… So, to finally have someone on her side felt good. Too good, so she had to snap herself out of it because he wasn't offering that kind of partnership. He'd done it in service to himself.

'We both know that isn't true. As long as you're carrying my child, your life is my business.'

The words sounded so full of sense that her feelings only spiralled even deeper. 'That doesn't give you the right to sweep in and start making decisions that affect the rest of it.'

He inched towards her, making her blood fizz and pop all over again. Serena could still feel where his arm had banded around her waist, as if the strength and heat of his skin had imprinted deeply, and she remembered how being pressed up against the hard, hot muscle of his body had made everything else she was feeling slip away and brought desire to the fore, as if she'd been turned upside down, yet had suddenly felt righted.

'I didn't hear you interrupting to tell your stepmother that I was jumping the gun, that we're not getting married,' he pointed out with a smartly arched brow, pausing for the observation to sit between them and rankle her further. Because it was true. She hadn't stopped him. 'And I think the reason you didn't is because you know that marrying me is the only solution available to you.'

Serena spun away from the all-knowing expression on his handsome face with an anguished exhale, knowing he was right on all counts. She didn't have any other options. She had consulted a legal expert. They could help, but it would be a protracted and expensive battle, and whilst it was a fight she would happily undertake, she couldn't afford to, not financially, nor, she suspected, emotionally. Not whilst she was pregnant and not when it was *now* that the twins needed her. Not in the years it would take for the battle to be waged and won.

No, if she wanted to be back in her siblings' lives, marrying Caleb was her only choice. Marcia would be far less troublesome if Serena had Caleb by her side. As much as anything else, she would enjoy having a stepson-in-law of such wealth and bearing. Was that why, as Caleb had pointed out, she hadn't interjected to correct him, even though the words had been on her tongue, hadn't pulled away from his snug grip around her waist, even as it had stirred memories, *yearnings*, that she would have preferred remained undisturbed? Not because his touch had penetrated every level of her being and rendered her helpless, but because for the first time in days she'd seen a chink of light on the horizon, felt a kindling of hope that she could right the wrongs and reunite with Kit and Alexis. Even if it meant compromising on the future she'd envisioned again and binding herself to this impossible man, wasn't it worth it to feel whole again? To be able to fulfil the last promise she'd made to her mother? Not to mention all the other advantages to her unborn child that she'd agonised over all night, wavering the more she'd considered…

'Fine. We'll get married,' she said, forcing the words out.

'I knew you'd come around,' he drawled with a smile

that was so wolfish that Serena's stomach quivered ominously, because at least when dealing with her stepmother, she'd known what she was letting herself in for. With Caleb, she had no clue.

But there was one thing she was absolutely certain of—she would not be giving up her freedom. He'd proposed a marriage in name only and that was what he would get, because the days of her living under anyone else's control were well and truly over.

CHAPTER SIX

IT DIDN'T, HOWEVER, take long for Serena to realise that she had very little control over what was happening. Only twenty-four hours after her reluctant agreement, she found herself in the South of France, having left London that morning on a private jet and landing a few hours later at a private airfield, where a car waited to transport them to the hilltop villa Caleb informed her would be home for the following weeks. A small contingent of staff greeted their arrival, ready to cater to Serena's every need and whim, but in spite of the beauty and luxury of her new surroundings, all Serena felt was overwhelmed. Powerless. The speed with which she'd been uprooted from her life and dropped into a whole new one had set her head spinning and her emotions struggling to catch up, feelings certainly not helped when in the same breath he informed her that he was leaving to attend to business matters, Caleb also told her he'd arranged for her to sit down with an event planner to discuss wedding details.

Serena had bristled at that. He had no right to make plans on her behalf and, really, she was in no mood to plan a union that she didn't want to happen. But had he asked her what she wanted? Of course not. And what details needed to be discussed for a wedding that was a formality anyway? Given the circumstances, Serena had assumed that it would be a discreet affair, with minimum fuss. However, within minutes of sitting down with the wedding coordinator, she discovered how flawed that assumption was. Per Caleb's instructions—words that made her bristles bristle—their wedding would be a showstopper, an event to proclaim their love for all the world to witness. Each detail had been more extravagant than the last, culminating with the arrival of the world-renowned couturier who had been hired to dress her for the big day, another of Caleb's executive decisions, even though it was customarily the bride's prerogative to choose her own gown. But the message was clear—she was in his world now, living by his rules and his expectations.

Out of the frying pan and into the fire.

It ignited an angry fire in Serena's stomach, and in spite of taking to the infinity pool in the hopes of relaxing, she tensed all over again. There was sense in marrying him, she knew that, but Caleb didn't seem to understand her agreeing to marry him didn't mean he had control over her life. Maybe she should have been clearer on that from the outset. That was something Serena would fix as soon as she saw him again, which she didn't imagine would be soon, as he'd told her he was in meetings until late. And that was how their marriage would unfold, she expected, with him running his global business whilst she lived her life at home. Serena hesitated on that thought, because Caleb hadn't actually specified how he planned on their conjoined life unfolding. He hadn't shared much of anything, really.

They'd passed the journey to France in relative silence. As soon as they'd boarded, Caleb had settled down to work, the head bent low over his computer emitting a very strong *DO NOT DISTURB* signal, and Serena had been happy to leave him to it, her feelings about him having become troublingly ambivalent overnight. As angry as she wanted to be at the way he had manoeuvred her to right where he wanted her, that emotion was hard to maintain when it had reunited her with Kit and Alexis. Instead, she felt a gratitude to him, and remembering the effort he'd made with her siblings had softened her feelings even more. She hadn't expected him to have any skill with kids, but not only had he charmed Alexis, he'd gently coaxed Kit out of his shell, and that had made her wonder at the father he would prove to be. It was a softer side of him that had reminded her why she had broken all the rules with him that night in Singapore, when she'd rarely been tempted to before.

So, she was glad at the resurgence of her anger. She didn't want to like him. Their situation would be easier if she didn't. Easier to keep from feeling anything remotely tempting or dangerous…

Like the sudden charge of crackling electricity that had her insides tightening and heat whispering over her.

Caleb.

He was back. She could feel the burn of his gaze awakening the parts of her that only he seemed capable of touching, stirring them into a fever. She ordered herself to ignore it, but found herself turning, regardless, seeking him out. Her eyes locked with his, and as they did a current shimmered through the air between them, so strong that she vibrated with the force of it. So strong that it scared her and she broke the connection, swimming to the edge of the pool and climbing out, reaching hastily for the robe she'd left on a nearby lounger.

'You didn't have to get out on my account,' he said, eyes on her, and she wished he would look away. Or even better, go away.

'I didn't.' She pulled the tie as tight as she could. 'I was done.'

'How did it go with the wedding planner?'

'Fine,' she replied, pausing to see if there was an apology forthcoming for the way he had thrown her into the situation with no warning and without asking her, but of course there wasn't. 'She seems to have a handle on everything. I, however, was a little surprised that we aren't just getting married quickly and quietly.'

'As in eloping?' he drawled with that maddening slant of his eyebrow that so eloquently conveyed his distaste. 'Eloping is all about secrecy, which implies that we have something scandalous to hide, which is the very image we're trying to avoid. A big, extravagant wedding is necessary for our purposes.'

Serena hated to admit, even to herself, that it made sense, because she really would have preferred something small and quiet, something that didn't resemble a real celebration. Because she hadn't just felt overwhelmed earlier, or aggravated. As she'd stood in a gorgeous, flowing white dress and saw herself as a bride for the first time, something else had stirred in her too, something soft and hopeful, almost *yearning*, something that had been dormant since Lucas and which she hadn't expected to ever feel again. Didn't want to feel now. And that had caused an upwelling of worry, because she needed her emotions to stay out of this, yet everything about this wedding was designed to draw out emotion.

Only Caleb hadn't asked what she would have preferred, had he?

He'd just taken it upon himself to make the decision about what was best and pressed ahead with it. Irrespective of what she thought.

'Then I'm sure you'll be happy with her work,' she said, feeling grateful for that fresh spike of frustration. 'But I would appreciate it, if in future, you would check with me before arranging a meeting on my behalf.'

'If possible, of course,' he replied airily. 'Since my meetings finished earlier than expected, I was able to pick this up for you.' Reaching into his pocket, he withdrew a small velvet box and placed it on the table that stood between them.

'What is that?'

'Why don't you open it and see.'

Apprehension bubbled beneath her skin as she reached for the box, her fingers trembling because she had a fairly good idea of what nestled inside. As much as she wanted to be able to breeze through the moment as if it was nothing, Serena was scared of the rush of emotion that could happen once she popped that lid open. She couldn't seem to manage the same emotional impartiality that Caleb conducted himself with, and as expected her heart jumped when she saw the diamond ring glittering up at her from a bed of black cushion. *Wow.*

It was so stunning that tears hit the back of her eyes, but she quickly blinked them away because the moment was as much of a pretence as everything else. And she didn't like that that bothered her. Didn't understand at all why it did, when the last thing she wanted was the vulnerability of love and marriage.

'Do you like it?' Caleb prompted when she failed to speak.

'Of course.' She could barely take her eyes off it, but forced herself to. 'It's beautiful. Any woman would love it.'

She was wary of saying anymore, of allowing her emotions too long a leash, especially in comparison to his cool practicality. However, the answer clearly didn't satisfy whatever response he'd wanted, as his jaw hardened and mouth firmed, eyes glittering with shards of angry obsidian. She could *feel* his displeasure too, even with the distance she was meticulously holding between them; it radiated off him in sizzling waves. 'Then put it on. It's not just to admire. You are required to wear it.'

Another command. Serena bristled at the instruction, but jammed it onto her finger, fixing him with her gaze. 'Happy, now?'

'Ecstatic.' Eyes narrowing, he subjected her to a protracted perusal, frustrated shadows cutting into the smooth planes of his face. 'I understand this situation isn't ideal, Serena. It isn't where I expected or wanted to find myself either, you know.'

'You think I don't know that? You made your regret

about what happened between us very clear that night in Singapore.' His nostrils flared as she threw that at him, and a line of intense colour scored its way across his cheekbones. 'And as if that wasn't enough, you then didn't even believe I was actually pregnant. You came to London intent on exposing me as a liar.'

Serena hated that it still hurt, that his opinion held such power over her. That she wanted him to see her as someone good. Someone who wasn't a regret.

'Put yourself in my position, Serena. With my wealth and status, I only questioned what any man in my situation would.' He sighed heavily. 'But you're right. I didn't handle the situation well, and you didn't deserve to be met with that. But when I got your email, I went into self-protection mode, and it was easier for me to believe that it wasn't true and to focus on that anger that made me feel, than it was to deal with all the feelings that accepting the truth would conjure.'

It was a moment of such startling and unexpected honesty that Serena's heartbeat faltered. It was her first glimpse of the man who lay beneath the impenetrable façade, and she wanted to see more of him.

'Feelings about how a family was never something you wanted?' she ventured tentatively.

He nodded stiffly, and the uneasy emotion spiking in his gaze seemed to hint at a wound that had never quite healed, a scar that he would go to any lengths to prevent inflicting on any child of his own. Her curiosity intensified.

'Did something happen to make you feel that way?'

He looked over at her, and Serena held her breath, her

heart racing with anticipation to learn more, to know *something real* about him, but with a blink, his gaze shuttered once again, and the abrupt change sent a chill across her skin.

'It's not important.' The words fell like bricks, re-constructing that wall between them that had, for a moment, felt like it was beginning to be dismantled. 'What matters now is that there is a child and we are going to be a family and that I do the best I can for both of you. It's not what either of us expected, but it's the situation we're in. I suggest you accept that. The sooner you do, the better off we'll both be.'

Her eyes narrowed, the words scraping against her overwrought senses, the disappointment at how quickly he had shut her out making her annoyance even more po-tent. 'You may be able to control everything else, Caleb, but you do *not* have command over my thoughts or emo-tions.'

He arched a brow, clearly disliking his command ca-pabilities being questioned. 'Is that so?' he drawled, gaz-ing down at her with such emotion brewing in his gaze that her bones actually shook.

Until that moment Serena hadn't realised that they'd been drawing closer and closer and now stood only an inch apart. They were so close that every frantic breath she drew in contained a heart-stopping trace of him, and in the glitter of his eyes she could read the intent to prove that, should he wish to, should he *choose* to, he could very easily exert mastery over all of her, just as he had that night in Singapore. Her breath locked in her chest at the prospect, as thrilled by it as she was scared. The light in his eyes deepened as they dropped to her mouth, eyes which seemed intent on devouring, and curse her, a part of Serena hoped that he would. Craved it desperately. Because she knew that the moment his lips touched hers, all else would cease to matter. Her frustration, her fear, her reality—all of it would be silenced by the exquisite texture of his sensual skill, by the possessive slide of his hands over her skin. There would only be oblivion, and right now, that was so very tempting to her.

An inch. That was all that was separating Caleb's mouth from Serena's. He would barely need to move his head to feel her lips yielding beneath his. And Caleb had no doubt that she would yield. The same flare of white-hot intensity that licked at his insides was dancing coaxingly in her eyes and humming in her blood. He could hear it. See it. The flutters of her pulse were so hard they were visible and it was *because of him*.

The intoxicating knowledge nudged him even closer to the kind of reckless behaviour he knew he needed to stay far away from. But, despite knowing that, in that moment, he found it difficult to care or believe in its imperativeness. He knew that the force of his longing was all the greater because it had been so long since he'd found sexual release. The only woman he'd wanted was the woman now standing temptingly close to him, her presence some kind of dangerous dare. And to finally slake that deep and vast hunger, to finish what they had started but not fully satisfied, all he needed to do was lower his head a single, tiny inch. But whilst that was what he wanted to do most of all, he hadn't entirely forgotten that it was the last thing he could allow to happen.

So, he summoned the discipline that had never been in such short supply as it was around Serena and took a step backwards. And then another. His blood continued to burn with the proximity of temptation, and even more alarming was the way he could feel that something between them had tilted. Not for better or for worse, but something that had been simmering since their reunion on the street in London, but which had not been acknowledged, had just flared too powerfully for either of them to be unmoved. To keep pretending it no longer existed. Even if it was the last thing he wanted to exist between them because there was no place for it in their relationship.

Their marriage was going to be an unemotional endeavor, and he needed to be sure Serena understood that. That he made the parameters clear now, at the outset, so that she didn't build pretty, romantic plans in her head and end up with her life in tatters, as Charlotte had. So that she didn't interpret any moments of unforgivable weakness on his part as anything other than exactly that—the very real needs of a red-blooded man around a beautiful woman, a woman who made him burn hotter and higher than any who had come before. Even after all this time, and all his efforts to put her from his mind.

He needed to keep it front and centre in his own mind too, especially now they were sharing the same home, because every moment spent in Serena's presence was a moment that threatened a loss of control that couldn't, *mustn't*, happen.

Only moments ago, he'd been felled by the sight of her in the swimming pool, the elegant shape of her back and the pale peach tone of her skin inflaming a desire that had stopped him in his tracks. His eyes had feasted on her, and he'd wondered if she was naked in the water and blood had surged south with the thought. He'd been hit with the thought of stripping off his suit and diving into the water to join her. But he knew better. And yet he hadn't been able to make himself continue on to his room, so he'd stood, drinking her in like a man starved of water, until the weight of his gaze had become too heavy and her head had turned and their eyes had caught and the connection that had zinged between them had been electric.

However, it had disappeared as quickly as it had struck, and instead of the fire and hunger that Caleb had wanted to see in Serena's eyes, there had been annoyance. Even the diamond ring hadn't sparked any pleasure, and it aggravated on a male level that whilst he had been affected, she hadn't. And he was being affected too often, and in too many ways. He'd let her believe that his dismantling of her stepmother had been done to press his advantage, which it had, but not entirely. He'd wanted to protect her too. She'd looked so fragile, so broken down by her stepmother that he'd wanted to be her white knight—not that there was anything to recommend him for the role—and rescuing her had felt good. Far better than it should. Which was far too much.

'You should shower and change. Chef Pierre will be arriving soon to prepare dinner.'

She blinked in surprise. 'You didn't mention anything about having dinner together earlier.'

'Well, I'm mentioning it now,' he snapped, his patience running low.

'And what about my feelings on the matter? Do I not get a say in how I spend my evening?' she demanded, the fire of her Italian heritage rising again as if from nowhere, and he hated that he found it so sexy, that it made him want to plumb the depths of her even more.

'No, you don't. There are matters we still need to discuss,' he riposted, seeing anger flash like lightning in her eyes again before he turned on his heel and walked away. Let her think of him as arrogant and controlling. It was better that way, better if she loathed him. It would help keep distance between them, distance he was struggling with. 'Be ready in an hour.'

CHAPTER SEVEN

SERENA LOOKED ANYWHERE other than at Caleb as they sat opposite one another at the table exquisitely set for two. Her body was still vibrating and her lips tingling with the want that had coursed through her and been left unsatisfied. She was so angry with herself for wanting the kiss so badly, and angry with him, for being able to step back so easily and then demanding she sit down to eat with him. Because with every interaction with him, Serena felt less in control of the situation, and even more worryingly, of herself.

'A contract is being drawn up and will be delivered to you before the wedding for your review and signature,' Caleb began, after their first course was laid before them. 'But I thought it would be a good idea for us to go over in person some of the main details of what our marriage will entail.'

'A contract?' The word caused unease to prickle along her skin, making her think of rules and consequences, reminding her too much of life under her stepmother. 'Is that necessary? This isn't a business deal.'

He dealt her a quelling look. 'That's exactly what this

is, Serena. A short-term merger so to speak. The contract just lays out all the particulars.'

She started to feel hot all over, trapped again. 'What if I don't like the "particulars" in this contract?'

'Since that's what we're going to discuss now, I don't foresee that being a problem. Now, the contract will state that we will remain married for a minimum of five years and then divorce at some point of our choosing after that, at which time we will share custody of our son or daughter equally and move forwards co-parenting.'

'Share custody?' Serena repeated, her hand settling protectively over her stomach.

'Unless you would like me to take primary custody.'

'No. If anyone should have primary custody, it would be me, the mother.' She had already lost one child and felt similar pain slicing through her at being separated from this one.

'But as already stated, I refuse to be apart from my child, and since you seem to feel the same, shared custody is the only option. Now, in terms of where we'll live as a family, I assume you won't want to leave London.'

'Of course not. Kit and Alexis are there.'

'Which I fully anticipated, and that suits me fine. With the European expansion, I had planned on relocating to Europe, and London is an ideal base. I've had my team researching properties and I feel this is the best. I'm sure it will be to your liking too.'

He held out the tablet for her to view the images of the chosen property, and although recognising that he'd shown a certain consideration in selecting London as their base because of her family ties, Serena still frowned at his instinctive autocratic ways. He said they'd be *discussing* things—only he didn't seem to know the meaning of the word!

'What do you think?'

'It's fine, but…'

'Very good,' he said, lifting the device from her hands and not letting her finish before continuing on with his agenda. 'As I mentioned, I'll travel often for business. The majority of the time I'll go alone, but on occasion you will be required to accompany me—and it goes without saying, play the role of loving wife. For example, the opening of the beach club here in a few weeks. You'll be by my side. There will be other events that you'll attend too—banquets, charity galas, social parties. My assistant will coordinate your calendar so you'll know in advance when and where you'll be required. Obviously, we'll take into account the pregnancy, especially as it progresses. No one is expecting you to exert yourself.'

No, just to pass over control of her calendar, as well as the next five years of her life to him, apparently. The disquiet spiking her blood grew hotter, and her head started to spin, overwhelmed by his high-handedness. 'Have you forgotten that I work full time?' she reminded him, determined to be heard this time. 'I can't be taking time off to travel and attend parties whenever you summon me.'

He looked back at her, untroubled. 'I'm sure we can work it out. You don't even need to keep working if you don't want to.'

'You expect me to give up my job?'

'No. But it's an option. I'll be providing for you financially now.'

'Caleb, that's generous, but I'm not sure I'm comfortable giving up that aspect of my independence. It's important to me that I'm able to take care of myself.'

'Even once the baby is born?' he queried. It made Serena wary to look that far ahead, not when there was so much time for things to go wrong. 'Because I don't love the idea of our child being raised by an army of nannies.'

Serena couldn't clamp down her annoyance at his he-who-shall-be-obeyed tone. 'So, you *do* expect me to stop working?' she demanded, reeling. 'Why did you say you wanted to *discuss* all of this, when you seemed to have made all of the decisions already, without so much as a conversation with me?'

'We're having a conversation now,' he responded, his coolness only making her feel worse because she was so overwhelmed. 'And I haven't made any decisions, I'm only expressing...'

'You're telling me *how* it will be,' she interrupted hotly, feeling like she was eighteen again and back in her bedroom, being told by her stepmother the rules and behaviours she was expected to adhere to, her world narrowing with each passing second. '*What* I will do and *when* I'll do it.'

Her frustration burned so hotly that her heart battered against her ribs as she saw her future unfold without her having any voice or autonomy in it. Again.

For a brief moment it had actually been within her power to write her own future, but now this.

Him.

She couldn't help but think of all of the things she'd lost and missed out on as her life had been steered by another hand, and her throat thickened as that feeling of powerlessness descended again. Truthfully, she didn't want a nanny raising her child either, but she wanted that to be *her* decision. Or an actual discussion between them. Not a law laid down that she was expected to obediently follow.

But he was so…domineering. She couldn't even loathe him for it, because he had used that resolute power to subdue her stepmother. Without him being the way he was, who he was, she would still be stuck in that hell of yesterday. She fought to remain calm, to stabilise the punching of her heart, but emotion was building, stacking higher and higher until there was only panic.

'Serena…'

'No. Stop talking. Please.'

But it didn't help. She pushed herself to her feet.

'Where are you going?' he demanded.

'I need a minute. I'm not asking,' she warned him as his mouth opened and she swept past him, taking the path down to the beach, called by the openness of the sea and sky, the way it stretched even farther than she could see, full of possibilities and no limits.

She'd never forgotten the stories her mother had told her of her time as a young artist in Rome and Paris and London. Serena had dreamed of following in her footsteps, even more so after she'd died, knowing it would keep the memory of her mother close, and she would have had the opportunity to live and work in Paris or Florence as part of her degree. It was that which had kept her focused, kept her grief over her father's passing and miscarriage from swallowing her completely. But right when she'd been on the cusp of it, Marcia had intervened, forcing her to choose between herself and the twins.

There had been no choice to make. Leaving Kit and Alexis was unthinkable, but letting go of her dreams had been so hard. It had been like letting go a piece of herself, and a piece of her mother. She wasn't losing anything as profound this time, but the emotion was the same nonetheless.

Serena didn't realise she was crying until she felt the teardrops drop to her chest. Lifting a hand to her face, it came away wet, but the release felt good, the pressure on her chest easing substantially. She had held everything in for so long, having to be strong, that this moment of privacy in which to break down was a gift, and she felt better for it.

'Are you ok?'

Serena sucked in a breath. The last thing she wanted was for Caleb to see her in tears. 'I'm fine.'

She had survived her stepmother and would handle this too. Because she wasn't a young girl anymore, frightened and fragile, and she wouldn't let this be the same. Wiping her face dry, she squared her shoulders and turned across the sand towards him.

'Let's go back to dinner and finish our conversation.' Calmer now, she had terms of her own to assert.

But as she passed by, Caleb's hand snatched out and seized her arm, halting her. His eyes raked over her face. 'You've been crying. You're upset. What's wrong?'

She tried to tug her arm free because his touch was scorching her skin and as that heat sank deep into her blood and her bones, her pulse skittered. But what shook her even more was the concern she read in his eyes, a concern that had long been absent from her life.

When she'd miscarried, Serena had had to take herself to the hospital. There hadn't been anyone to hold her hand or stroke her hair as she'd tensed in battle against the indescribable discomfort. There had been no one's shoulder to cry on, no arms to comfort her when the doctor had delivered the bad news and no one to take her home and tuck her in bed to rest and mourn. She'd had only herself to rely on, and going forwards, that was exactly what she had done.

It had been sink or swim and she'd refused to drown. To give her stepmother the pleasure of watching her flounder. That was how she'd lived the last five years, not looking for care and affection from others, because she knew she couldn't count on it being given. It had been hard and lonely...but less painful. So, to see it now, in the last place she would have expected to find it, in Caleb's face, was disarming, and even more surprising was that she wanted to tell him—everything. To not have to be strong and guarded and just...be.

'Serena? Tell me.'

'OK,' she said, following the feeling, even though she had no idea where it would lead. 'I thought I was finally going to get to live my life on my terms. To be in control of my life, at last, but instead...there's you. With your commands and expectations and contract. Telling me what I will and won't do. And I don't want to be told what to do and who to be anymore.'

'I'm not telling you what to do,' he blustered, but a quick look at her tear-streaked face had that conviction deserting him. 'Or at least, I'm not trying to.' He looked bewildered by the accusation, horrified that she had even for a second imagined that he was trying to control her. 'Serena, if that's how it seems, I'm sorry. I appreciate that I can be somewhat domineering…'

'Somewhat?' she quickly cut in, her brow arching.

'OK, a lot domineering,' he amended. 'It's what my life, my role, demands of me. But I don't ever want you to think that I want to control you. That's the last thing I want.' He stared down at her, his gaze weighty, working to assimilate this new, explosive information. 'It was your stepmother, wasn't it? The person telling you what to do before?'

Serena nodded. 'It was the only way I was able to stay in Kit's and Alexis's lives—by adhering to what she wanted, living by the rules and standards that she set. Everything from where I worked to how I dressed, to who I was friends with was dictated by her.'

Horror leached into his expression. 'Serena, I would never try to tell you how to live. Not at all. I hate that I've made you feel that way. I'm sorry. God, I…' Drawing in a breath, he ran his hand over his face. 'All I was trying to do was to banish some of the uncertainty from this situation we're in and make sure we're on the same page moving forwards. Not for a second did I think you would feel dictated to. That's the last thing I intended. Please tell me you believe that.'

His dismay was so apparent, so genuine that it was easy to believe his taking charge emanated from a conscientiousness and not a will to control. 'I believe you.'

His relief was palpable. 'I still don't understand why your stepmother would treat you that way?'

'Because...' Serena stopped as soon as she started. There was no way for him to understand without knowing the whole story. But it was a story that out of fear and shame she had never shared with anyone, keeping it bottled so tightly within her. But how could he understand otherwise? And, much to her surprise, she wanted him to understand. And surely, he had a right to know. Taking a breath, she began again. 'Because she didn't trust me to behave and not create another scandal like the one I caused when I got pregnant at eighteen.'

Shock rippled through his silver eyes. 'You were pregnant before?'

She nodded, anticipating his next question. 'I miscarried at nine weeks.'

'Serena...'

'That's why she did it. Because she didn't think I could be trusted and that I could be a bad influence on the twins. And given that I did fall into your arms within hours of meeting you and fall pregnant again, maybe she wasn't wrong.'

'First of all, you have no reason to feel any guilt or shame about what happened between us,' he asserted strongly. 'It was natural and wonderful. And when I said it shouldn't have happened, I meant me taking someone less experienced than me. *You* were never a mistake. And secondly, I don't care about your stepmother right now. Only about you.' His throat worked, and she could see how affected he was by her admission. 'Serena, you lost a baby.'

'Yes.' And now that she had uncorked that bottle, she could feel it all rising up within her, that tide of feeling she had always been so afraid of. Scared to speak of in case others shamed her as Marcia had, or blamed her as she blamed herself. But, looking into Caleb's expression, so full of compassion, she felt safe to speak. 'It was awful. I was alone in this hospital room for hours and I just felt like… I'd failed.'

'Yor stepmother wasn't with you?'

'No,' she scoffed. 'Things between Marcia and I got worse after that, but they'd been bad before. Not just because of her,' Serena admitted. 'I never made it easy. I didn't want her in our lives where my mum should have been. I accepted the marriage because my father asked me to, because he said Kit and Alexis needed a mother, but I never wanted her there and we never got on. I never felt like she liked me. She loved the twins from the moment she met them—I think she liked that she could make them hers, that she would be the only mother they knew—whereas I was my mother's daughter through and through. And I looked so like her—the woman my father had loved first and still loved. Whilst he was alive my dad was our go-between, advocating on each of our behalf's and smoothing over the tension he could see. But once he was gone…that tension just ballooned. Nothing I did was right. And when she learned I was pregnant, she was furious. Scandalised and ashamed. And when I miscarried…all she had to say was it was probably for the best.'

Tears rolled from her eyes and she was taken aback when Caleb pulled her into his arms. 'She should have supported you better. She owed you that.' His voice contained a trace of anger. 'Regardless of how you behaved, you were a grieving girl. She was the adult. She'll never hurt you or shame you again. I promise.'

The words were delivered with such conviction that Serena couldn't do anything but trust them and, held so tight against him, she even felt secure enough to peel herself open more 'I'm scared that the same thing is going to happen again—with the baby,' she admitted in a whisper. 'I try not to think about it, but it's in my head. There was no reason for why it happened last time… which makes it worse. If there was something I could do or avoid doing…but I just feel like I failed. That I somehow caused it to happen.'

'I don't think it works like that,' he murmured, detangling from her, but continuing to holding her by the arms as he looked down into her face. 'It just wasn't meant to be, as hard as that is to accept. Did you like Dr Newman?'

'Yes.'

'Good. We'll make an appointment for you to see her as soon as we return to London, and after that you'll see her as often as you want to, OK. Whatever it takes for you to feel comfortable and reassured. And if you're ever worried that something is wrong, tell me. I don't care if it's the middle of the day or the middle of the night. We'll do whatever it takes to keep this pregnancy safe.'

'Thank you,' she murmured. It was the exact reassurance she needed, and she didn't know how he'd known that, but as she looked up at him, she recognised the haunted look in his eyes, the urgency of not wanting to lose anyone and feel that sting of loss again. Had he lost someone too, she wondered. That could explain why he'd never wanted a family, because loss went hand in hand with love. Maybe that was that why he kept such a tight hold on everything as well, trying to prevent a repeat of whatever he had suffered.

Caleb presented such an impenetrable front, but the past few hours had shown that he was vulnerable too.

'And moving forwards I'll try to be less domineering. But I really did just want us both to know where we stand going forwards.'

Boundaries were important to him, Serena realised, as much as her freedom was to her. He liked clear and defined lines that didn't get smudged. It was what had unpinned him in Singapore, that he had strayed from his norm with her, crossed some invisible line, and he needed those lines to be comfortable. But why? What was he so afraid of happening?

'I get that now.' She sent her eyes up to his face, feeling thrumming through her as she did. 'I know it hasn't seemed so, but I am grateful that you're here, that you want to be involved and grateful for what you did with Marcia. I have Kit and Alexis back because of you.'

'It's admirable—all you sacrificed for them.'

'I could never leave them. They were only seven years old at the time. They'd already lost both our parents. They couldn't lose me too. And I promised my mum, when she was pregnant with them that I'd always be there for them. I couldn't let her down.'

'You haven't.' He was quick to issue that assurance. 'Your brother and sister are lucky to have you, Serena.

And our baby is lucky to have such a strong mother.' His expression grew serious, and caught between the sunlight and growing shadows, Serena saw a whole new plane of Caleb's face, saw the whisper of vulnerability that flashed and then slowly faded. 'I have no idea what kind of father I'll be, so I'm glad they have you.'

Her heart caught. 'Are you scared? Of being a father? Is that why you were reluctant to accept that I was pregnant?'

He was slow to answer. 'I'm scared of making mistakes that I've already made before.'

The words were so stark, and his expression, as he emitted them, so bleak that her stomach knotted. 'What could you have possibly done that was so bad?'

He looked away, out into the encroaching darkness. 'I hurt someone once. In every way a person can be hurt.'

'Who?'

'Her name was Charlotte. We were…involved.'

'I thought you didn't have relationships,' Serena murmured, her heart faltering with a spike of envy.

'I don't.' A warning seemed to shoot from his eyes. 'I didn't then either. It was a casual thing, at least to me. But since then, since her, I don't even do that.'

'What happened?'

'I was young and reckless. Impossible.'

'You're still impossible now,' she murmured with a small smile, being granted one in return, but it was only half-hearted.

'I was worse back then. I lived a charmed life. I was used to getting everything I wanted, and the moment I saw Charlotte, I wanted her, so I did what I always did—

pursued her until I got her. She was only in Melbourne for the summer. She had no knowledge of my lifestyle, how I cycled through women, and I never explained it to her. I was just having fun, but she was falling in love with me, talking to her family about us living together and getting married.' He paused, regret writing itself into every line across his face. 'When Charlotte realised that I had no notion of a future with her and never had, she was crushed, as she had every right to be. She lost it right there in the club, screaming at me that I'd led her on. Then she stormed out.' He exhaled and closed his eyes and, seeing how arduous it was for him, Serena reached out, touching her fingertips to his knee, letting him know she was there. 'I should have followed her. I should have run after her. Every time I replay that night in my head, I do. I chase after her, stop her. I get her home safe. But I was careless and selfish, and I just let her leave. She went to another bar, had too much to drink and then got in her car to drive home. And then she rammed the car into a tree.'

Serena's breath stuck somewhere in her throat, but she kept her eyes fixed on Caleb.

'She broke her back and a few other bones. She needed to have surgery on her spine and then months of rehab. The company she'd spent the summer interning for had been so impressed that they'd offered her a permanent position, but she couldn't take it, not with her injuries. Her future, everything she'd worked so hard for, was set back years. Because of me.'

The words fell like a hammer blow and he looked away, a line of deep-seated shame scoring its way across his cheeks, and Serena marvelled at that burden that he made himself carry.

'No, not because of you. What happened to her was awful, but it wasn't your fault, Caleb.'

'Of course it was,' he insisted sharply. 'She was too smart, too level-headed to have done anything like that before getting involved with me. But I hurt her so badly that she forgot herself entirely.'

'Yes, you hurt her. But the decisions that caused the accident were hers.' How could he not see that? 'You weren't responsible.'

'I wreaked havoc on her life, Serena. And her family's life. You should have seen the worry and pain on their faces at the hospital. Because of me. And the things they said...they were right.'

'They were angry, Caleb. Upset and scared. They needed someone to blame and lash out at. But you're not to blame. You shouldn't be punishing yourself for what happened.'

He looked away again, and Serena inched closer, even though what she really wanted was to hold him as tight as she could, the way he had held her. He had condemned himself for what had happened, without seeing that a man without a conscience wouldn't care. He would have moved on, absolved himself and forgotten. The fact that he carried what had happened meant that he'd never been, not even for a second, the reckless man he believed himself to have been. But he'd consigned himself to a prison of his own making as punishment for a crime he was determined to believe he was guilty of.

'It's as you said—you were young. You made a mistake. But you're not the worst thing you've ever done.' Did he not think he was deserving of love or a happy future? Of course, she realised, this was why he limited his involvement to the briefest period possible, painting thick lines around himself. Everything he hadn't done with Charlotte. 'That's why it's important to you that everything is neat and clear between us? So, there'll be no misunderstandings?'

'Yes.'

Serena nodded, wishing she knew what more to say, but as she searched for the right words, Caleb glanced at his watch and shifted. 'It's late and you've had a long day. You should get some rest.'

She didn't want to agree. She wanted to stay locked in the moment with him, both of their guards down so that it felt like the beginning all over again, but she was exhausted, not to mention emotionally drained, and the fact that she wanted to stay meant she definitely needed to move. Because she had liked getting to know the man that Caleb was beneath his strong surface a little too much. So, distance was necessary now, to reset after such an emotional evening and pull her emotions back to safe ground. Because the last thing Serena needed, or wanted, was to get caught up in him, in their relationship, and Caleb had been clear on not wanting that either. *I don't have relationships.*

He'd marry her, but he wanted nothing else. And Serena was determined to want nothing else from him either.

CHAPTER EIGHT

THE MUSIC FROM the quartet changed, signalling the arrival of his bride, and Caleb's shoulders tensed, the magnitude of the moment striking him squarely in the chest despite his efforts to pretend this was just another day.

It will be fine. You have this all under control, he assured himself in response to the apprehension thudding through his veins and thwacking against his heart like a drum as he thought back to the starlit moments he and Serena had shared on their beach just a few days ago, and how close they had drawn together in those moments.

Closer than he should ever have allowed...

But her confessions about her traumatic miscarriage and difficult relationship with her stepmother had touched a part of him that was normally untouchable, and once again, he'd felt sore at how much she'd endured, whilst also marvelling at her resilience and strength in refusing to give up. Feeling so much for her had shaken him, and before he'd really known what he was doing, and before he could silence himself, he'd been telling her about Charlotte. *Why?* He'd asked himself that question over and over again since, and as much as he'd tried telling himself it had been as a cautionary tale, a warning to Serena about wanting too much from him, he couldn't make himself believe that. No, it was almost if he'd wanted to share it with her, to be as open and brave as she had been with him and offer up a part of himself, deepening their connection instead of halting it, which was bizarre to him because that was never something he'd wanted before. So, what had come over him in that moment?

And when she'd said he wasn't to blame…for the first time Caleb had wondered if that could be true. Her assurance had felt stronger than his guilt, and for a moment he'd wondered if he wasn't destined to always cause pain, if he didn't have to carry all that guilt with him into his future as a father. And husband.

Not that he wanted a real future, not with Serena, not with anyone. That was a decision he'd made long ago, long before Charlotte, after witnessing and experiencing the destruction that love could unleash.

The proud beaming man sitting in the front row with his wife of eight years by his side was not the father that Caleb had grown up with. Back then, his father had been broken and distant, tormented by the loss of his wife and unable to offer his son anything because there was nothing in him to give. Hollowed out himself from being deserted by his mother, Caleb had longed desperately for something, *anything*, from his father, and the ache when he hadn't received it had been messy and tormented. Agonised, hopeless feelings had rattled in his body all day and night long—feelings he had worked hard to suppress and lock away and which he had no interest in unleashing again, and until now, until her, they'd never felt in any danger of being unlocked.

But Serena evoked more feeling in him that anyone else had ever managed to. And not because she was carrying his child and he felt a sense of responsibility towards her—he'd already tried dismissing it as that—but just because of who she was. That was what was most disconcerting—that for no apparent reason she exposed the soft spots that still existed within him. The pieces that could be made to feel.

To hurt.

Parts of himself that he didn't want to exist, and keeping himself so busy in the preceding days had been as much about closing down those weaknesses within him as it was about preventing a repeat of anything that had arced between them on the beach—that sense of closeness and connection and the yearning for more of it— *especially* that.

Because there was no place for it, not in their marriage and certainly not in his life. The last thing he wanted was closeness and confidences. He was happy holding everyone at arm's-length and didn't want Serena to override his usual emotional reserve.

It had happened twice now…there couldn't be a third time. He wouldn't let there be. Their marriage was a practical endeavour after all, and after a lifetime eschewing emotion, it shouldn't be difficult to heed the warnings filtering down from his brain that counselled—*urged*—caution. Distance.

He had managed it successfully the past few days,

resetting their relationship to what it should be, and saw no reason for the lines to blur again.

Sensing Serena's approach from the buzz running through the guests, Caleb turned his head, eager to prove that the past days distance had worked and he could look at her and remain detached… Only for the sight of her to punch every last whisp of air from his lungs.

She was…exquisite. Breathtaking.

Beyond retaining the services of a renowned French fashion designer and instructing them to provide a dress that endorsed his narrative of a whirlwind, fairy tale falling in love, he hadn't much considered how Serena would look. Now he wished that he had in some way prepared himself, because then maybe his heart wouldn't be beating quite so fast and the fabric of his custom suit wouldn't feel quite so tight as his body swelled with sexual hunger.

The dress, whilst every inch the romantic and elegant creation he had specified, clung to her like a second skin, revealing to his appreciative eyes the changes wrought by the pregnancy. Her hips had more curve, and her breasts were unquestionably fuller. Whilst aware of his promise to maintain distance, physically as well as emotionally, suddenly he craved the taste of her in his mouth more than anything else, craved the intimacy of her essence lingering on his tongue. Caleb imagined drawing the material of the dress down and sucking her nipple in his mouth and an answering heat sliding sinuously in the pit of his stomach, before shooting south with all the force of a bullet.

Later, he thought excitedly, and it took a moment for awareness to strike that there wouldn't be a later. Because this was not a real wedding. How had he forgotten that, even momentarily?

Serena reached him, her caramel eyes meeting his with a nervousness that she was clearly trying to fight, and he reached for her hand, squeezing it tight, belatedly telling himself he did so as part of the show.

The officiant started to speak, and Caleb tried to listen to the words, but was prevented by the feeling pulsing steadily beneath his skin. It only intensified as Serena pledged herself to him, her voice rattling ever so slightly with nerves, and he returned the sentiment with a possessiveness that he knew should not have been beating quite so fiercely in his chest but which refused to calm. It was acceptable for other men to feel that way on their wedding day, but not him. This was not a real wedding, after all. Not a real marriage.

'With great happiness, I declare you husband and wife. You may now kiss your bride.'

Caleb smiled down at Serena, ignoring the surge of delight the officiant's words had prompted, and curled his arm around her, drawing her in slowly to deliver the gentle kiss that would be appropriate and risk-free. However, the moment his lips met hers and he was struck with her intoxicating scent, all thoughts of slow and steady faded.

Instead, there was hunger and need and those flagrant forces conspired to drive his tongue into the warm cavern of her mouth. He devoured the taste of her, thinking only of staking his claim so completely, of doing what he hadn't allowed himself to do, to even really think of doing. Serena shuddered against him, but didn't resist. One of her hands flattened against his chest, the other sliding around his neck and with that tender touch, the flames roaring in his gut raced along his veins, the kiss gaining heat with each second. He angled her head for better access, drawing more of her elemental response from her as he hugged her even closer to his pounding body. Then he heard it, the sound of applause exploding around them, and finding some remaining vestige of control, Caleb eased his mouth from hers.

Keeping hold of her trembling body and avoiding her dazed gaze, he turned to face their cheering guests. But as they walked back down the aisle, showered by thousands of flower petals, behind the smile etched on his face, Caleb's brain whirred with troubled whisperings. Suddenly he was wondering if this marriage was going to be as manageable as he kept telling himself.

'It's time for our first dance, Mrs Morgenthau.'

Serena glanced at the hand that Caleb held out, fear skittering along her veins at the heat that would take hold when her skin brushed against his, when he pulled her against his body and held her close. But Evie was right beside her, watching, and everyone else was watching too, so Serena summoned a smile and, drawing up as many barricades as she could, placed her hand in his, letting him lead her to the centre of the dance floor.

The hand that settled on her back scorched, burning through the thin fabric of her stunning gown, and she fought with all of her might not to melt with instant desire. But that was a battle that she'd been losing nearly all day long.

Serena had started the day a nervous wreck, her stomach cramping as she sat through hair and make-up, antsy with the thoughts of what lay ahead even though she knew it was the right thing. But, in spite of that, more than once she'd wanted to turn and run as she'd waited to begin her walk down the aisle. Had still been thinking about it as she made her way to the altar, but then her eyes had locked on Caleb—seeing him properly for the first time in days—waiting beneath the abundant arch of fragrant white flowers, and her feelings had shifted.

Nerves continued to ripple beneath her skin, but they were threaded with heat, and the longing to run was no longer to run away, but *towards* him. Because in the tailored suit superbly fitted to the tall musculature of his body, and looking more darkly, impossibly handsome than usual under the beam of sunlight, he embodied every dream her head had once been filled with, everything she had once wished would be waiting for her in her future, and remembering how he had held her as she'd cried out the pain and shame that she'd been carrying for years, she'd felt inexorably bonded to him. Serena's heart had quickened even more as he'd settled his striking eyes on her, watching her as if she was his every dream come true too, and for a tiny second, she had fallen under the spell of the moment, believing that it was real, that in spite of all the hardship she'd been dealt, she had finally found her way to happiness. But that had snapped her out of it, because she knew happiness never lasted. Whenever she'd thought she was approaching a happy and settled place in the past, the bottom always dropped out of her world with more hurt or loss. In that way, her arrangement with Caleb was ideal, because she knew exactly when the end would be and wouldn't have anything invested emotionally to feel that loss like a physical wound.

Or so she told herself. Yet, since their conversation on the beach, her feelings for Caleb had been evolving.

He'd been so understanding, and so open in return, and for the first time it had really occurred to Serena how he must be struggling with the enormity of what they were doing too. Logistically. Emotionally. He invested so much energy in keeping people at arm's length, afraid of hurting them the way he'd hurt Charlotte, but he'd hardly hesitated at bringing her into his life and that had to be costing him something.

Hard as she had tried to not think about him, to not watch for his return to the villa, Serena did. Too many times she'd caught herself wondering about the man that he was and the scars that he bore, wanting to know even more. Which was completely illogical, because she'd agreed to give him her hand, not her heart, and yet the thought of him never failed to make her heart beat faster.

But still, the thought of her heart becoming involved filled her with dread. She didn't want to give someone that degree of power over her, and she was reminding herself of that a lot, and that their relationship wasn't real. And that she didn't want it to be.

And that heat building and pulsing at your breast-bone—is that not real either?

Pushing that awareness, and the questions it raised, out of her mind, Serena concentrated on keeping her smile in place, keeping her eyes on Caleb, starry and dreamy, as if this was everything she had ever wanted as they progressed through the ceremony, even as she worked to root herself as firmly as she could in reality, plant her feet so deeply she wouldn't lose herself to the charade again.

But then…that kiss.

Her eyes had widened as the officiant invited them to seal their vows with a kiss, having conveniently overlooked that part of the ceremony, but she had no time to dwell on it as Caleb lowered his head. She'd assumed it would be something brief and sweet. After all, he'd made it clear, with words and actions, that there would be nothing between them. But there had been nothing chaste about what had exploded between them.

The second his mouth had touched hers, heat detonated in her like a firework. Prising her lips apart, his tongue had curled against hers, stroking the inside of her mouth, and she'd been helpless, unable to fight her instinctive response, that hungry neediness that surged from deep within her to see her fist her hand around his neck and hold him close, pleading with her body, her fingers, for him to never, ever stop what he was doing.

But of course, he did. Because he was only acting and so ended the kiss easily, whilst she had felt every single pulse of it in every inch of her body.

Events were something of a haze after that. She remembered Caleb leading her back down the aisle to applause, his hand tight around hers. She remembered the wedding planner stealing them away for photographs and being painfully aware of Caleb's every touch, and of the panic when each touch penetrated that much deeper, evoking an even deeper quiver of longing. Though she continued to smile and pose, Serena had grown more anxious by the second, fretting that she had tied herself to someone she had little hope of resisting, and no amount of rooting herself in reality would be enough to combat that vital and visceral attraction.

It hadn't been problematic when she was annoyed by him, but now there was nothing to prevent those feelings from flooding her, and Serena became even more blisteringly aware of that as his body brushed purposely against hers, and her face rested close to the nook of his neck, inhaling that bergamot scent straight off his skin, skin she was close enough to touch. To…

Her thoughts scattered as his fingertips caressed the bare skin of her back, and she felt the bones in her knees threaten to give way. She didn't know how she was going to get through this. How she would survive the next five minutes, never mind the following *five years*?

They stretched ahead, long and ominous, day after day of longing for the husband she shouldn't want and couldn't have. And what about the nights? Sharing the same home, same space as him, teased every day by his scent. It had been hard enough the last few days, even though Caleb had rarely been present, but now with this new fervent desire pulsing in her veins—a beat that felt as if it would never stop, it would be impossible.

'You're tense,' he observed, breath as warm as fire brushing her ear.

'Sorry,' she murmured, trying to wipe her mind clear. She was thinking too much about feeling too much, and she needed to stop doing both.

'Is it your stepmother? I saw the two of you talking. Did she say something to you?'

He tensed, primed to leap to her defence and Serena found herself smiling at that even as she shook her head. 'It was just a brief conversation. I thanked her for coming and for bringing the twins. She complimented the wedding and the dress and you. I think I've actually done something she approves of.'

'After the way she treated you, it should be her worrying about earning your approval, not the other way around,' he ground out, his anger on her behalf igniting sparks in his eyes. 'I still can't believe how she treated you for all those years. But maybe...maybe in her own mind by being so tough on you she was trying to protect you.'

'I doubt it,' Serena retorted sceptically. Just because good intentions had underpinned Caleb's domineering delivery didn't mean the same was true of her stepmother. But then she really considered his words and saw the slight possibility in them. She remembered how Marcia had tried to warn her about Lucas; at the time Serena had assumed she was just being Marcia, but maybe she had been trying to protect her. 'But then again, maybe you're right,' she acquiesced. 'I've never really thought of it that way. It was always so uneasy between us that I just assumed everything she did came from a bad place. And, come a certain point, I started to think that I...'

'Thought what?' His gaze probed hers. 'That you deserved it?'

'Yes,' she admitted tearfully, realising just how much she had internalised it all. She had to take a breath, feeling unsteady. 'I did mess up. I didn't show the greatest sense, or that I deserved to be trusted.'

'Serena, you were a young girl who lost her mum and then her dad and you were grieving. You suffered so much in a short space of time. It was your stepmother's job to understand that and be there for you and support you. It was her who failed you, not the other way around.'

The moment felt like a release, as if something she'd carried for far too long had just whooshed out of her. It was so powerful that tears slipped down her cheeks, and Serena made the decision in that moment to choose to believe that some of Marcia's tough treatment of her had been in an effort to protect her, and now she was ready to move on from it as best she could. She'd carried pain and frustration for long enough and wanted to begin this new chapter without that baggage. And as long as Kit and Alexis were in her life, Marcia would be too.

She smiled up at Caleb. 'Thank you.'

'For what?'

'For being kind. And supportive.'

He brushed away the falling tears with his thumb. 'I told you—this may not be the most traditional set-up, but we can make it work.'

She nodded, believing in that. 'I'm not sure I'll ever like being dishonest with people about our relationship though. Lying to Evie today has been awful, especially because she's so happy for me.'

'I'm sorry. I know that it's hard. Hopefully with time it will get a little easier.'

'As easy as it is for you? Because you don't seem to be struggling at all.'

A light smile touched his mouth. 'It's not without effort, I promise.'

Oh. The words stung and it must have shown on her
face.

'I didn't mean that way,' he breathed quickly, pulling
her harder against his body when she wasn't sure he'd
meant to. 'There's no hardship in touching you, or holding you. Only in stopping myself from doing more of it.'

The words struck her heart like a bolt of electricity,
and as her eyes lifted to his with surprise, she saw the
same shock in his. Although she knew she'd be wiser to
let it go, she couldn't. Because as much as she didn't want
to give him her heart, her body rejoiced at the thought of
being seized by him.

'I didn't think you were interested in…more,' she said
carefully.

'I'm trying not to be.' The fact that he didn't deny
wanting more with her made her blood fizzle. 'But you're
not making that very easy,' he added, casting her a glance
filled with longing. It was the most unguarded she had
ever seen him and seeing that power she possessed over
him too sent a thrill snaking through her. 'Don't worry.
I don't plan on acting on it, or renegotiating our arrangement. It's better if it remains as it is.'

Serena didn't disagree, and yet there was a part of
her that wondered *why*? Which was a bad thought. An
unwise one. It was hard enough exercising control of
her thoughts without further confusing them with sex,
and yet there was always the possibility that giving into
their chemistry would bring clarity and not confusion.
If they leant into the sexy, edgy energy and satisfied the

beating needs of her body, maybe she could stop fretting that her feelings were more than desire. She knew Caleb wanted to keep the waters between them clear, and she did too, but provided they both agreed it was about attraction and pleasure only, would it be the worst thing if the lines blurred a little?

Yes, it would, a voice in her head screeched, and Serena quickly shook the crazy notion from her mind, questioning frantically where it had come from.

For the remainder of the dance, she guarded her thoughts carefully, relieved when the song ended and she was able to step away from the temptation of her husband. At least temporarily…

When they arrived back at the villa, Serena was exhausted. Not from the celebrations, but from the effort of resisting Caleb and controlling her own thoughts and reactions to him, especially after his revelations about desiring her… That had shaken everything in her, and even though she'd kept a tighter rein on her thoughts, ever since then their interactions had felt even more charged. Even now, when the pretence was over and she should have been able to relax, she was still achingly aware of the sensual tension oozing in the air between them, making it heavy and hot as it brushed against her skin. It wasn't helping that with their arrival back at the villa, she kept thinking of what would be happening were this a real wedding night, her throat thickening as she did, because a part of her was aching for that pleasure-filled release.

'I guess this is goodnight then,' she said, breaking the

heavy, crackling silence as they hovered in the open plan living space, their bedrooms at opposite ends of the villa.

'It's not that late,' Caleb mused. 'Stay up for a nightcap with me?'

It was the last thing she'd expected him to say, and though the invite was delivered innocuously, it somehow seemed laced with...danger. Breathing quickly, Serena contemplated an answer, letting her eyes slowly journey towards his, and as they met, the truth of where the night would end if she agreed shimmered between them. Her heart launched into her throat. It was only a handful of hours ago that he'd said he had no intention of acting on his feelings, but she sensed they'd gone beyond what he could control now. She didn't know how it had happened, or when, but she could taste the inevitability of it, feel the pulsing life force of their mutual desire. It needed only a single spark to catch alight and send them both up in flames, and she wasn't sure she was ready to be caught in that inferno.

Are you prepared to not experience it either?

'I'm not sure that's the best idea,' she admitted with a quivering smile, unable to forget the many reasons to resist. The safety in resisting. 'I think I should just go to bed.'

'You're probably right,' he conceded with a wry smile of his own, his eyes lingering on her, as if savouring his last look of the day. 'Goodnight, Serena.'

'Goodnight Caleb.'

On trembling legs, she turned and walked to her bedroom. Even once alone, her body continued to jostle and she had no idea how she was going to sleep, not with such ferocious want beating in her blood. Quickly, however, Serena realised she had a more immediate problem. She couldn't reach the fastenings at the back of her gown to take it off, and no amount of manoeuvring of her arms was helping. Asking Caleb for help was her only choice, but she had only just managed to walk away before and wasn't sure she'd be able to do so a second time.

Why do you need to? You're both feeling and wanting the same things. And neither of you are looking for it to mean more.

Serena was tired from the effort of denying herself. She had spent so much time being held back, and not just by her stepmother's rules, but also, she could see now, by herself. The events in her life had taken a toll on her, knocking the fearlessness out of her and impressing on her the advantages of caution. She'd been scared of making more mistakes and bringing on further hurt and disappointment. But something had happened today. She'd let go of the belief that she had screwed up and the walls that had been holding her in had shattered, releasing all the pain and fear that had plagued her, and she could see more clearly now.

Serena wasn't the young vulnerable girl she had been, desperately seeking love and family. She wasn't going to make the same errors. She was older now. Wiser. She'd craved a future in which she lived for herself, decided for herself, and if she was completely honest, she knew what she wanted. All she had to do was trust that she could handle it. Reach for it...

Taking a breath, she pulled open the bedroom door and returned to the living area, only to find it empty, but carried forwards by the new, empowering certainty within herself, she ventured to the other side of the house.

The door of Caleb's room was slightly ajar, and with another breath, she knocked lightly. 'Caleb?'

'Yes? Come in.'

The richness of his voice sent nerves skittering across her skin as she pushed open the door to his private space. A sole lamp lit the spacious room, the low lighting creating an intimate impression and that was before her eyes found him. When they did, Serena stilled. He was midway through getting undressed, his black trousers riding low on his lean hips and his chest bare, all hard muscle and gold skin for her eyes to gorge on. She remembered all too well the feel of him, but the sight of him…that was something else entirely. An even hotter heat exploded in her middle, engulfing her from head to toe, and all the moisture in her mouth evaporated as her eyes traced the faint line of hair bisecting his torso all the way down to where it disappeared into the band of his trousers.

'You need something?' he asked when she didn't speak.

Levering herself out of her stupor, Serena nodded. 'I can't reach the fastenings at the back of the dress, and I was hoping you could help.'

She couldn't control the warble to her voice, not when she could taste the danger of this moment, feel her feelings ready to catch fire with one single touch that she craved so desperately…

'Of course.'

As Caleb came towards her, she turned to offer him her back. Her breath shifted, quickening with the anticipation of his touch, and her stomach was tightening, almost to the point of pain, with the longing that ascended from so deep inside of her. Gently, he brushed her hair to the side, and as he did so his fingers brushed the sensitive skin of her neck. It was like being electrocuted, sparks of feeling arrowing in each and every direction. Shivers travelled across her skin as his fingers moved to undo the tiny buttons, his warm breath fanning over her, his body so close that she could feel…*everything.*

Strength. Heat. Temptation.

Surrender.

As his fingers moved lower, it got harder and harder to breathe. The dress was unfastened enough now for her to complete the task, but she made no effort to move and Caleb didn't remove his hands; instead, they slipped confidently beneath the fabric, settling on her waist and Serena swallowed a gasp at the blissful meeting of flesh. *Yes. Touch me. Take me.*

His fingers spanned outwards, creeping upwards to brush the base of her breast and this time she was powerless against the shudder that rippled through her. She had never wanted to be touched so desperately in her life, for her breasts to be cupped and caressed, stroked and sucked.

'Caleb…' She sighed, pressing back against him in invitation and turning her head for his mouth to claim hers, a kiss that, when it began, was unrestrained.

His tongue stroked the seam of her lips and then delved into her mouth, and with a sigh that seemed to be ripped from the deepest recess of his body, Caleb pulled her tightly against him. The gown slipped to the ground and his hands roved down her body in a slide that was pure possession. Excitement bubbled beneath her skin, liking it, wanting it. Needing it. To be claimed by him. To belong to him in every way possible. There was no one else she could imagine committing such surrender to. And this was…essential. Imperative. There was no other way to describe how it felt between them. She had to seize this gloriousness with him whilst it was here, because happiness never lasted, did it?

His firm mouth demanded more, demanded everything she had to give, and Serena offered it without hesitation, turning in his arms and clinging to him as the current building between their bodies threatened to sweep them both away. With another rumble from deep in his chest, Caleb scooped her into his arms and carried her to the bed, his mouth never leaving hers.

He tumbled her on to the softness of the covers, and Serena curled herself around him as snugly as she could, her blood beating with an unknown rhythm, whimpering as he pulled away, but only briefly and only so he could rip at his trousers and then he was covering her again, naked, his skin hot to the touch and as he fitted himself onto the cradle of her thighs, her body filled with so many wants and wishes, so many feelings, she wasn't sure how she didn't explode.

'You're so beautiful, Serena,' he breathed, the rise and fall of his chest heavy, as though she was too much to truly take in. 'So beautiful it's driving me crazy.'

The final words were delivered on a breath of desperation, and then he was lowering his head in worship, burying his face in the valley of her breasts so the embers simmering low in her stomach exploded into a full-on wildfire. His hands moved to palm her breasts, but they had become so sensitive that at the tiniest amount of pressure, she gasped, and Caleb pulled back, alarmed.

'It's OK,' she assured him breathlessly. 'They're just really sensitive right now.'

A soft light burned in his eyes. 'I'll be very gentle then.'

And he was. Beautifully, exquisitely gentle. He caressed her almost reverently, stroking her with fingers as soft as a butterfly's wing and where he would have used his thumb, employed his tongue instead, licking and sucking her into the warm heat of his mouth and the tenderness of his ministrations only seemed to send their power arrowing deeper into her so that she was quivering beneath him.

'Caleb,' she pleaded, the stars flashing before her eyes with such brightness she was half-convinced she could reach out and touch them.

His only response was the flash of a smile as he drew his line of teasing kisses even lower down her body, blazing a path over her stomach and lower again to where she had never been touched. Even if Serena had possessed the breath to protest, she wouldn't, because his mouth on her most secret cavern felt like the ultimate way of giving and belonging, and there was a relentless tattoo striking right there, which only throbbed with greater insistence as his mouth neared. And then his mouth was on her, his lips and tongue moving with synchronised perfection and in a matter of moments Serena was soaring, spinning higher and higher out of herself and it didn't once enter her mind to be scared of the plummet back to earth, because she knew that Caleb was there to catch her.

Caleb had never seen a sight more beautiful than Serena trapped in the grip of her quaking release. She sparkled with the orgasm tearing through her, and as the ripples subsided long enough for her to open her eyes, and they locked on him, her smile was as dazzling as rays of sunlight.

'That was incredible,' she breathed, reaching for him to press, fast, eager kisses to his lips.

'I am nowhere near finished yet,' he promised, his chest flooding with the pleasure he'd given and all that he still intended to bestow and with a single move pinned her beneath his weight.

Surrender had never felt so good. Thinking only about this moment and nothing else. For the first time in a long time, it was the impulses of his body leading the way instead of his brain, and his body wanted this—closeness, pleasure. *Serena.* He had known the moment they returned to the villa that he didn't want to fight anymore. *Couldn't* fight anymore. He had been fighting all day, and after too many moments holding her close and being teased and tempted by her softness and her scent, his hunger for her was too great to be denied. Another night without her seemed…impossible. And had he known how spectacularly eager and responsive she would be beneath him, he would have lost his battle hours earlier.

Caleb drew his lips across her mouth, before moving down her neck and chest, over her stomach and then to the arch of her thighs, dropping open-mouthed kisses back up her body. He would have kept on kissing her, tasting every inch, but his impatience was insistent, and with the way she was arching and pulsing under him, Caleb couldn't wait a moment longer to sink his hard length inside her, and the welcome he received, her muscles stretching and tightening around him like a hug, was beyond his greatest longing. He wanted to hold steady, to relish that moment of reunion after craving it for so long and so fervently, but he simply couldn't. He had to move, compelled by the emotions powering through him. More than everything he had already acknowledged feeling for her, more than protectiveness, more than lust.

She shuddered out his name as he started to move, slow and deep, and with each surge, the sensations unfurling beneath his skin and throughout his chest tautened and deepened. It felt like drowning, in the best way possible. Pleasure saturated him, and as she craned her mouth to reach his, the sweetness of her exploding on his tongue was an aphrodisiac unlike any other he'd ever known. His climax began to build, too soon but unstoppable. And as Serena hit her peak, her cry the most joyous, breathless sound he'd ever heard as he delivered her to a world that was uniquely theirs, Caleb's climax ripped through him, his roar of release drowning out the sounds of her fulfilment before he collapsed on top of her like a ship wrecked on the shore.

CHAPTER NINE

SERENA WAS THE first thing Caleb saw when he opened his eyes the next morning. Her face soft and beautiful in sleep, her lips curved with contentment. He would have been content to lie and watch her a while longer, but the warmth filling his chest and the stirrings that had absolutely nothing to do with sex were making his mind uneasy, so he turned away and slipped out from beneath the covers, careful not to wake her.

He didn't regret last night, not at all, but entertaining thoughts of lazing away the morning in bed with her was not OK. Giving into them even less so. Just because she was now his wife didn't mean he could abandon all of his usual practices; in fact, it probably made them even more important, especially with the way Serena could so easily get under his skin. He couldn't do anything that encouraged her to believe that their marriage was now, or ever could be, *more*.

He didn't want to feel deeper yearnings within himself either, not when those kinds of feelings only caused emotional chaos, the kind that had reigned over his childhood. He'd never been able to forget the long days and longer nights of agony that came from being deserted by his mother and all but ignored by his father—a pain that had felt it would never end.

He'd found a way to live that was chaos-free and he wasn't going to abandon that now, not when the stakes were higher than ever with a child of his own coming into the world. So, he took himself for a swim, cleansing himself of all yearnings in the clear, warm water before settling into his office and turning his focus to work, ignoring the uncomfortable thoughts of Serena waking up alone after such an incredible night together.

He didn't know how long he'd been burying himself in work when there was a small knock on the door, and looking up, he found Serena standing in the doorway, her sleep-tousled hair tumbling around her shoulders. She was wearing only his shirt. His heart thudded. 'Are you busy?' she asked before he even found his voice, his eyes too busy lingering on the line where the hem of his shirt met her slender thighs, his eyes drifting down her endless legs.

'Just sending emails.'

'They must be very important to be sending out the morning after you get married.' She strolled towards him. 'Considering you're the one concerned with our marriage appearing real, I would have thought you'd realise that looks a little suspect. Working is definitely not what a man besotted with his new wife would do' She came around to lean against the desk, her legs directly in his eyeline, and he had the sense she knew exactly the temptation she was. 'Unless you're really in here hiding?'

'Why would I be hiding?'

There was a flash of insecurity in her eyes that he

knew had been put there by him. 'Because you regret what happened between us last night?'

'No. Last night was incredible,' he assured her, wanting so badly to touch her, but knowing that one touch would lead to another and another…and then he'd never be able to stop, so he dug his hands into his pockets instead.

'So, you left bed at the crack of dawn because…?'

He took a breath, the answer an easy one because it was the truth. 'Because we agreed to this being a marriage in name only, and I don't know that blurring those lines any more than we did last night is the best idea.'

She absorbed that with a steady expression. 'Because you're worried that I won't be able to separate sex and emotion, and I'll get the wrong idea and end up hurt the way Charlotte was?' she questioned astutely. 'Or because you're worried that *you'll* end up hurting again?'

'What do you mean?' he demanded, startled that she'd come so close to the truth he'd never exposed.

'You were hurt by what happened too,' she said softly. 'Not in the same way, but you've carried the guilt and pain of it for years. It's understandable that you wouldn't want to feel that way ever again.'

'You're right. I don't,' he admitted. He didn't want to feel anything. That was preferable to the everything he'd felt as a boy, the constant agitation of his heart, the huge cavern in his chest and the endless yearning that had driven him crazy until he'd shut it down by cutting himself off and removing love from the equation. For good.

'Then let me assure you that's not going to happen.' She met his eyes with firm insistence. 'I'm not going to let it happen. My eyes are open to what this is, Caleb. What our marriage is. What last night was. And it's enough for me. I don't want anything more, anything real.'

'You don't?' he asked, surprised, because he knew that at one point in time Serena had known such a happy life. He'd seen it when she talked about it, and in his mind, it was natural that she'd want to have that again. It was what most women wanted, wasn't it?

'Maybe at some point I did. I can see how tempting it would have been to recreate what I'd known when I was small and I had my parents. But a lot has happened since then,' she said with a sad tilt of her lips, 'and I know now that anything real comes with risk, and I don't want that. I don't want to lose anyone else. I can't go through that again.' He watched as she touched her hand to her stomach without realising it. As familiar as he was with loss, and as much empathy as he had for her, Caleb knew he really couldn't comprehend how great her fear of loss must be, not after experiencing so much of it, but this was the first time he'd ever heard her allow it to define her. As pleased as he was to hear it, because it suited their arrangement—even meant he could bend the rules a little—it also made him sad. 'Not after my parents and Lucas and the miscarriage. Those days worrying that I'd lost Kit and Alexis reminded me of how much I don't want that risk in my life.'

'Lucas?' he questioned, the name having stood out to him. 'Who... Was he...?'

'The father of the baby I lost, yes. Also, my boyfriend.'

'You didn't mention him before,' he said tightly, not liking the thought of the faceless stranger from her past.

'For good reason.' Serena sighed. 'He took off after I told him I was pregnant, crushing my heart in the process. It was a week later that I miscarried.' The anger that Caleb felt on her behalf was extreme and overrode all need for distance, and he reached out to her, sliding an arm around her waist. 'I think that's why I was so hard on you when you first showed up. I was projecting, expecting you to do the same. But I was wrong. You're a thoroughly better man than he ever was.' Her hands splayed against his chest; her amber eyes warm as they looked into his. 'I know you've spent a long time not believing that, and I know that I don't know who you were back then—maybe you were everything you say—but I know who you are now. Someone good and generous and protective. A man who does the right thing, who takes care of the people in his life.'

'Always. I'm not going to walk away, Serena.' He was vociferous. Wanting—needing—her to believe it, to never be plagued by that fear with him. 'I want you to know that and trust it. We've both had to endure the pain of that and I'll never do that to our child.'

Caleb's words caused Serena's heart to stutter. 'Someone left you too.' She saw his frustration that he'd spoken without thinking. His hand dropped from where it had settled and he retreated a step, but she wasn't going to let him push her away. He'd tried that once already this morning, leaving her alone in bed, and for a moment it had worked, before her understanding of him had kicked in and she'd realised he was trying to reset after breaching his own lines. She knew how important boundaries were to Caleb. He told himself it was about keeping others safe, but she sensed it was as much about protecting himself. And maybe this was why. 'Who?'

'My mother. She walked out the door one day and never came back.'

Serena's mouth dropped open. She knew his mother hadn't been at the wedding. He hadn't told her, but she'd realised it on the day, and whilst she had intended to ask, there'd been so many other things clamouring for attention.

'How old were you?'

His smile was sad. 'Three'

Serena gasped. 'Three?'

'It's a blessing really. I don't remember her, or her leaving.' But the look on his face spoke of a curse and not a blessing. From his body language, it was obvious he wanted to shut the topic down, maybe even regretted telling her, but Serena had so many questions. This was a trauma they shared. Was this why he'd been so understanding and supportive of her, because he knew the emotional scars she bore? But, then, why hadn't he let her support him in return? She knew the struggle it was to find people with similar experiences who could understand. She'd felt so alone with hers until Caleb. She didn't want him to feel alone either.

'Why did she leave?'

He shrugged, shaking away the shadow that had descended over his expression. 'I don't know. I don't think motherhood made her very happy.'

'She never tried to reach out to you?' He shook his head and her heart jammed somewhere in her throat. 'I'm so sorry, Caleb.' She reached for him, sliding her hand up and over his arms, the muscles bunched tightly.

'You don't need to be sorry,' he said curtly, before gentling his tone. 'I told you, it's not something I remember, so it didn't affect me a whole lot.'

Except he was talking about it, and the memory had been roused by her own tale of abandonment, so he clearly felt something. 'You may be able to get away with spinning that line to other people, but not me. I know how it feels to not have a mother. And I know the toll it's taken on Kit and Alexis, not remembering our mum. The scars it's left'

'There's a big difference between my situation and theirs. Their mother died. She was taken from them, and you. Mine made the choice to leave.' He said it with such a heart-wrenching starkness that she wanted to fold him into her arms and hold him as tight as possible for as long as possible.

'That's why it was so important to you to be involved,' she realised, the wound she'd sensed in him but not been able to see. 'Why you insisted on us marrying, so our baby would grow up with two parents.'

Caleb barely acknowledged it, but Serena knew she was right. Knew that regardless of what he said, it had affected him, only maybe in ways he didn't want to acknowledge, ways he didn't know how to express. She wished he'd told her sooner. It would have gone such a long way to explaining his earlier insistence, maybe making it easier for her to accept, to understand his actions as protective and not controlling.

'It's also why you avoid relationships, isn't it?'

His eyes were veiled as they lifted to her. 'I think that's enough sharing for one morning. We have plenty of time to get to know these things.' But it was obvious he didn't want her to know them, didn't want to dwell on his mother and the scars it had left. Or how to heal them. *And it's not your job to heal them,* she reminded herself. *You're his wife in name only.*

But that didn't mean they couldn't be close, or friendly. Surely their situation demanded it, and if helping him enabled him to be a better father to their baby, it wasn't only about him. It was about all of them. But he was right—there was time for that.

'If we're not going to talk, we'll have to find something else to do. I have one idea,' she mused, burning with the thought of him taking her again. Last night hadn't been anywhere near enough. She wanted more time to explore his body, to explore the heat shimmering between them. Last night, Caleb had shown her what it was to matter, to be wanted and hungered for. Worshipped. She wanted her chance to revere him too. 'Unless…' It occurred to her then that maybe he didn't want her body as much as he didn't want her heart. Maybe as enjoyable as last night had been, it hadn't blown his mind the way it had hers, and he was using this as a convenient excuse. She was inexperienced after all—maybe she hadn't satisfied him. Maybe that was why she had woken to an empty bed.

'Unless what?' he prompted, raising an eyebrow.

Serena swallowed the insecurity bobbing in her throat. 'Nothing.' She lacked the bravery to expose that much of herself to him. And if he tried to deny it, that would be…too awful. But he advanced towards her, taking her chin between his fingers and tilting her head back until she was trapped in his gaze.

'You question if I really desire you? Even after last night?' She couldn't answer, there was too much emotion crowding her brain. 'Serena, if you knew how hard it is to see you in only that shirt right now, to see the outline of your body, to breathe in your scent and not bury myself inside you…if you could feel what being this close to you is doing to my body, you would know how very much I do want you.'

His voice was low and rough, sexy, and Serena trembled beneath his words, her blood humming as if she was being subjected to his touch. 'What are you doing?' he asked as she reached out.

'Feeling what I do to you.' He didn't let go so much as he loosened his grip enough for her to free her hand herself, and she laid it gently against his bare chest, right above his heart. The rapid beats pulsed against her palm, hard and insistent. It stole her breath, and with her heart leaping in her throat, she slowly slid her hand lower, tracing over the ridges of his stomach and slipping beneath the waistband of his pants and onto the erection that was throbbing with heat and steel. His breath hissed out, but that only encouraged the slow strokes of her hand.

'Enough.'

'No. Not enough.' Flicking her thumb across the tip of his erection, she watched his control shatter, watched him fight it. His eyes darkened to gunmetal. She couldn't tell if his resolve was weakening or strengthening, but she knew her own will was strong, as strong as it ever had been. This was her marriage as much as his, and having found her voice again, her confidence, she wanted to keep using them.

With a growl, his mouth crashed down on hers, his hands on either side of her face, holding her captive as his tongue plundered mercilessly, soaking up every ounce of her hunger. He growled again, not getting enough, and hauled her against him, lifting her shirt and pressing his burning hands to her hungry flesh. The more he touched and tasted, the greater Serena's hunger grew. With hands and tongue, she urged more, faster, and Caleb obliged, pinning her against the nearest wall and lifting her up, and with a single thrust of impatient possession, buried himself inside of her. Her climax hit hard and powerful, the long and glorious shudder wracking him too, and he buried his face in her neck, breathing loudly.

After a few minutes, he moved, carrying her with him. 'Where are we going?'

'To bed.' His eyes glowed like obsidian. 'And I'm warning you now, we won't be leaving it for a while.'

'This is beautiful.' Caleb watched Serena's delight with enjoyment as they sailed into the sheltered bay, their destination the picturesque harbour ahead. 'Where exactly are we?'

'Villefranche-sur-Mer.' He smiled, extending his hand to help her off the yacht once they had docked.

It had been five days since the wedding, and this was

the first time they'd left the villa—the first time Caleb
had let Serena get clothes on—but she'd mentioned her
desire to explore the region, and Caleb had been more
than happy to make it happen. It wasn't behaviour he
would normally have engaged in with a woman, but with
Serena's assurances that she understood the lines between them and wasn't going to develop feelings for
him beyond the desire they shared, he saw no harm in
the deviation. He liked seeing her happiness, particularly
knowing that she had known too little of it, and whatever pangs of unease he experienced about breaking another of his norms, he dispelled with the argument that
being seen enjoying typical honeymoon activities would
only help their marriage charade. Additionally, building
a good relationship now, from the outset, would enable
them to co-parent better in the long term, even once their
marriage was over, except looking ahead to that point in
time sent discomfort drilling deep into his chest.

Pushing the thought away and keeping hold of Serena's hand, he guided her up from the harbour, past the
waterside restaurants and into heart of the town.

'It's like stepping back in time,' she mused as they
strolled the medieval streets, the sun warm on their skin,
the day stretching easily ahead. Caleb relished that feeling of freedom, of not having to distract or restrain himself. 'How did you find the town?'

'I explored the region pretty extensively when I was
looking for the perfect South of France location.'

'You don't have a team who do that?'

'I do. But I like doing my own research too, ensuring
that everything fits with my vision. And with this being

our first European location, it was important that every-thing was absolutely perfect.'

'And is it? Absolutely perfect?'

'Almost,' he smiled. 'It will be by the time we open.'

She turned her face up towards him, the light catching in her hair so she shimmered. 'Do I get a sneak peak of this beach club before it opens?'

Caleb looked back at her in surprise. 'Do you want to see it before the opening?'

'Of course. You've been working so hard—I'd like to know what you do every day.'

Her interest sparked more pleasure than it really should, but he was too preoccupied with the thought of showing it to her, sharing it with her, to truly care. 'Then, of course. I'll take you one day.' And because felt a lit-tle too happy about doing so, feeling himself edge into deeply personal territory, he qualified it as part of their charade—that, of course, a husband would give his wife a preview of his work.

'Is your father excited about the European expansion?'

'He is. That and the new generation of Morgenthaus have conspired to make him a very happy man at pres-ent.'

Serena stopped to admire an ancient church. 'Will you expect our son or daughter to take over the com-pany one day?'

'I'll want them to be part of it, if that's what they want. But I wouldn't want to ever bully them into it, make them feel as though they can't explore other avenues.'

'The way you felt?'

'Yes. So please, if you ever see me doing that, feel

free to step in.' He only realised what he'd said after he said it, looking forwards that many years and seeing them together. *Wanting that?* He dismissed the thought. Of course he didn't want that. He never had. *But* if the situation worked to their advantage, then there was no reason the five years couldn't be extended. 'But I do like the thought of having our child to pass it all onto, and share it with. Lately, there's felt a greater purpose to all the work I do. It's always felt somewhat about the past, continuing the legacy of my father and grandfather. Now it feels more about the future—about what I can leave to our child.' He realised he was smiling as that feeling of purpose filled him.

'I know your father has stepped back now, but did you enjoy working with him?' asked Serena.

The question, such a complicated one, caused strain to his chest. 'My father and I have never had the easiest relationship.' She didn't look surprised, but she was no stranger to parental tension, was she? She would understand it better than most, and maybe that was why he continued speaking when it was a vault he never normally opened. 'It's been that way for as long as I can remember. We never quite recovered from my mother leaving. Or *he* didn't, I should say. He threw himself into work to deal with it, or *avoid* dealing with it, and was rarely around, so we never established any kind of father-son bond.'

Memories rose quickly, of how his father would never quite meet his eye, and on the few occasions he did, seemed to look right through him. So aware of the absence of his mother, Caleb had been so desperate for his father's attention and affection that he could still feel the memory of that desperation squirming within him and quickly worked to lock the memory away, disliking the feelings ready to spill free and cause havoc within him.

'Was that why you resented him pushing you into the business?' she asked as they turned into another narrow street.

'Probably,' he admitted. 'To suddenly see me and demand my capitulation after fifteen years of ignoring me was a little hard to swallow.'

'He ignored you?' Serena breathed, shocked.

'Like I said, he struggled a lot after she left. He… blamed me somewhat, I think.'

You. She left because of you, Caleb.

'Why would you think that?' Caleb couldn't bring himself to say the words, but the answer was conveyed in his silence. 'Did your father say that?'

'Only once,' Caleb responded quickly, feeling protective of his father in spite of it all, because he knew how pained he'd been by his mother walking out, so it had to have been ten times worse for his father, who he knew had loved her deeply, 'and he'd made quite a dent in a bottle of Scotch by that point. I don't think he even remembers it.'

'You never asked him about it again?'

'It wasn't a conversation I was in a hurry to revisit.'

'You don't believe that's true, do you?'

He shrugged lightly, keeping his gaze fixed ahead. 'I've wondered. I saw photos of them together and they seemed happy, so something obviously went wrong once they had me.'

'Caleb, there could be a hundred reasons why your

mother left. None of them to do with you,' Serena said urgently. 'I know how easy it is to let stuff like that go inward, but you can't think like that. Not when the chances are your mother left for her own reasons.' She ran her free hand up his arm, dissolving the tension in his biceps with just her touch. 'You really don't remember anything about her?'

'No. And after she left, my father removed everything that was a reminder of her.'

Her fingers curled around him. 'I'm sorry.'

'You must have plenty of memories of your mum,' he said, neatly redirecting the conversation because he had no desire to dig any deeper, and Serena nodded. 'Tell me about her?' he asked, knowing from the way her voice changed that she loved speaking of her mother and hadn't had enough opportunity to do so.

'She was beautiful. Vivacious. The most fun person in any room, with the biggest smile and most stunning laugh. Sometimes, I still think I can hear it.' Her smile was wistful. 'She could make even the dullest day fun. And the way my father used to look at her...he adored her.' She paused, hesitated, looked up at him. 'I think that was the worst thing about living without her, that the house seemed so quiet, so lifeless, as if all the happiness had gone, which in a way it had.' She looked down at the cobbled ground. 'We muddled on, my dad and I and the babies, but it was never the same. It's probably why whenever I do feel happy now, I'm always waiting for the bottom to fall out of it.'

'You can be what she was to you, to our baby though.'

'I hope so. She was a really good mum. I know Marcia always thought she sounded too spontaneous and lively to be a good parent—which I think was always why it hurt so much when she accused me of being the same way, because she really was the best. She had a joy that not many people have. I was actually thinking that if we have a girl, we could name her after my mum. Not necessarily her first name, maybe a middle one...but it would mean a lot to me.' Her nervous flow of words ended with a look of hope.

'What was her name?'

She smiled. 'Francesca.'

Caleb nodded. 'That's beautiful. It's a perfect idea.' Her smile was brighter than the sun, and Caleb could only stare, captivated, delighted at making her beam so widely.

Leaning down, he stole a kiss from her lips. 'What was that for?'

'I just wanted to.'

And he wanted to do it again, and again, to have that sweetness of her mouth permanently on his to lips to savour. Instead, he threaded his fingers with hers and resumed their stroll, uneasy thoughts buzzing around the edges of his mind, because he'd told himself he would get her out of his system, had justified their intimacy on those grounds, but the ways he craved her were only intensifying. And that wasn't the worst of it. The worst was that in certain moments, he was no longer sure that getting her out of his system was something he wanted at all.

Serena hadn't thought the day could get more enjoyable after their morning exploring the charm of the medieval town, but as midday approached and they continued on their journey around the coast, they sailed into a secluded cove to enjoy a luxury picnic lunch on the narrow curve of sand. They were sheltered from any view by the most spectacular wall of rock, and azure waters glittered ahead of them as far as the eye could see.

The picnic had been provided by one of the restaurants back in Villefranche-sur-Mer, boasting rustic baguettes with pâté, quiche Lorraine, a pan bagnat, a selection of fruits and miniature lemon meringue tarts, the taste of which exploded on her tongue. She couldn't have painted a more idyllic day and was touched that Caleb had gone to so much trouble to arrange it. However, Serena took care to remind herself that it wasn't done solely for her or from the goodness of his heart. He had, no doubt, considered a sighting of them on a typical honeymoon outing would consolidate their fictitious love story. She wasn't under any illusions as to how important it was to him that the world perceive their marriage as real, that they ensure that protection for their child, and now that she knew about his mother leaving him as a small boy, she understood it a lot better. He wanted to ensure that their child never experienced any of the insecurity or vulnerability that he had felt. Knowing that he had ever felt that way made her heart sore.

Serena had wanted to ask him more about that time in his life, to uncover just how significantly his mother's leaving had impacted him. In those circumstances his relationship with his remaining parent would have become all the more significant, but it was clear from his words, that his father had been too lost in his own agony to have any time for Caleb's. Was that why Caleb didn't want anything real? His view of love and relationships had been coloured by the breakdown of his family, seeing only loss and anger and pain where there should have been love. Had he felt too much negative emotion himself to want to risk opening up again? And to have blamed himself…it was little wonder Caleb had felt so guilty about Charlotte when in his mind that was the second time he'd been responsible for a tragedy, and even less surprising that he'd shut down even more afterwards. But maybe, with a little time and encouragement, he could get comfortable opening up again, for the sake of their child if nothing else. Serena hoped that he'd heard her when she said it wasn't his fault, but she wasn't sure. And she knew any further questions would be out of bounds, and the last thing she wanted was to upset the closeness they had created.

Caleb was not a man who yielded easily, but he had yielded on that, and she definitely didn't want that to change, she thought, watching him emerge from the sparkling aqua waters from his swim, looking like a deity who'd descended from another world. Her eyes clung to him as he ran up the sand towards her, sleek, bronzed and muscled with droplets of water clinging to every ridge of hard muscle. Her mouth ran dry as feeling exploded along her veins and gathered low in her stomach.

How was it possible that a man, mere flesh, blood and bone, could be so spectacular? Her body grew hotter, that single glance conjuring a need, a hunger, that was unlike anything she'd ever known. Her body yearned for his touch, for the feel of him above her, just as her mouth ached for one of his deep, devouring, kisses, and thinking it, her nipples pulled tight and taut, her core *throbbing*.

Almost as if he knew the effect he was having, his eyes gleamed as he dropped down on top of her, tempting her with his closeness and lightly kissing her lips, smiling as he did, teasingly pulling back as she leaned in for more.

'Come in the water with me—it's beautiful,' he said in between light kisses.

'I'm rather enjoying the view from where I am right now. Maybe in a little while.'

'Now,' he commanded. 'You can either come willingly or...' He let the slow smile imply the rest.

'Or?' she prompted laughingly.

'Or I'll just do this.' Scooping her up in one effortless move, Caleb sped back towards the water, not stopping until they were chest-deep. Her laughing ceased only when his mouth covered hers, and he didn't break the kiss until she was gasping for air. With her legs wrapped around his waist, she felt the hard press of his erection and almost groaned, the feel of it sending shock waves crashing through her and igniting the same scorching need as always at her core. Serena hadn't known that desire could be so beautifully painful. Nor could she quite believe that he wanted her as much as he did.

At least for now. She knew there was no promise of permanence. At the most she'd have a few years of the sensational pleasure he could deliver. At worst—until his desire waned.

It shouldn't hurt so deeply. It was what she had agreed to and all but instigated, after all. But perhaps, at times, she hadn't been as watchful of her thoughts as she should have been, gazing into the future and seeing life in a way she hadn't been capable of for the longest time. Seeing herself and Caleb and their child, a little family. Growing together, happy together. But it wouldn't be that way forever, would it?

Comforting rather than scolding herself, Serena accepted that it was understandable, but cautioned herself against indulging those daydreams going forwards. She had to keep a tighter rein on her thoughts, and perhaps her feelings also. Happiness was a beautiful thing, and she was enjoying this period of it, but it never lasted. The bottom always fell out eventually, and she had to remain pragmatic to be sure she didn't end up crushed when it did. Because she'd been broken before, in so many ways, and had meant it when she said she had no interest in that happening again.

'If the plan is to make it to Monaco at some point this afternoon, shouldn't we be getting back to the yacht?' she prompted, with that in mind.

His eyes drifted to her lips. 'Fifteen more minutes isn't going to hurt,' he said, seizing her mouth eagerly as beneath the water his hand slid between her legs, under her bikini, and she arched, clinging to his shoulders even tighter, resistance impossible as she became his whole focus.

Fifteen more minutes definitely, she conceded as his fingers stroked her to realms of incredible pleasure. But would that be enough? Would there ever be a time when Serena could say enough? Now that she knew Caleb's touch, how deeply it could penetrate and move her, would she ever be able to stop wanting him? She'd meant every word of her promise when she'd made it—to both him and herself—but Serena was no longer so sure it would be quite so easy to keep.

CHAPTER TEN

'THERE THEY ARE—the newlyweds.' As Serena and Caleb made their way through the front door of the property, they were greeted by the welcoming smiles of their hosts, Thierry and Mathilde Clement, faces that Serena vaguely remembered from their wedding. 'We're so pleased that you were able to come and celebrate with us, interrupting your honeymoon, no less.'

'We wouldn't have missed it,' Caleb smiled smoothly, showing none of the nerves that were writhing in Serena's stomach as they embarked on their first public appearance as a married couple. The evening was important to Caleb, and she didn't want to do anything to disappoint him. 'Would we?' Caleb asked, gazing down at her with eyes that sparkled like starlight, and her heart leapt in response.

'Not at all. I cannot wait to see all the work you've done here. Caleb told me you've been renovating for two years, so I'm sure it's going to be spectacular.'

'Your wife is as generous as she is beautiful, Caleb,' Thierry remarked smilingly. 'There's no question why, after a lifetime, of bachelorhood you wasted no time putting a ring on her finger.'

'What can I say? Serena got under my skin the moment we met and I just couldn't let her go.' Serena glanced up at him, warmed by his words. She knew they were a key part of their narrative, but there was a sincerity to them and an ease to their delivery that made her wonder if they could be more than just a soundbite. If they contained some kernel of truth. She knew it was true for her, that Caleb had affected her, in spite of her dogged pretence to the contrary, right from the start, but was it possible that she burrowed just as deeply under his skin? The thought thrilled her, sparking hope that was dangerous, but too potent to be extinguished. 'I was always told it would happen one day and I never believed it, but…here we are.'

His eyes stroked over her again, rousing tingles everywhere, and as their gazes caught, a deeper and richer light started to smoulder, something that seemed to speak only to her, the deepest, most secret part of her. A message that only she would see and understand. Everything in her responded. Was that another sign of his feelings changing, deepening in spite of what he had said about not wanting anything real or was he just a far better actor that she was? Playing the performance of his life for their hosts to eat up?

Serena didn't know. But she wanted to know. It *mattered*. And yet it shouldn't matter. She shouldn't care. She certainly shouldn't be feeling cold and wobbly at the thought that he was only pretending when it was what they'd agreed. But when he looked at her like that, when his fingers moved against her waist in that subtle, tender, exquisitely powerful way to soothe her nervousness, because he knew without her having to say anything that she was nervous, everything felt confused and she couldn't keep her mind, or her heart from forming questions that she'd be safer and smarter not asking, not wanting to ask.

But the thought that he could possibly feel more for her, that it wasn't all a pretence—that was dizzying. Electrifying. Heart-stopping.

'Serena,' Caleb prompted and she realised she'd been so deep in her thoughts that she'd lost the thread of conversation.

'I'm so sorry. I was too busy admiring everything, and I stopped listening for a second. Forgive me.'

'Please admire away,' Mathilde encouraged. 'That is why we invited you. Admiration and compliments, as many as you wish, none too grand.' Serena smiled at the other woman's playfulness, liking her immensely and feeling a little more at ease. 'How about a tour, my dear? You and I can get to know each other better, since you'll be regular visitors out here with the new beach club. You can tell me all about how you and this glorious man met.'

As Mathilde drew her away, she was aware of Caleb tensing and keeping hold of her. 'Do I not get the tour too?' he asked with a laugh.

'If you are unable to part from your bride for all of thirty minutes, then by all means join us,' she offered airily.

He pretended to consider for a second when Serena knew by the look in his eye his mind was already made up. 'I think I will. Thirty minutes is far too long for us to be apart.'

Mathilde flashed them an indulgent smile. 'Young love. So beautiful.' Her eyes moved to Thierry with fondness. 'I remember when that was us, *ma chérie*.'

'I would say it still is us,' he drawled, dropping a brief kiss to her lips before she beckoned them to follow her.

Caleb stayed close, his chest pressing against her back, his hand resting on her waist as though he couldn't bear for their contact to be severed. Serena's heart soared with the thought, but remembering her pledge to keep a tighter rein on her thoughts, she brought herself back down with the caution that it could be nothing more than foolish, wishful thinking to indulge in the romantic notion that he couldn't bear to part from her, when really it was all for show, Caleb playing role of a besotted and attentive husband? And if she let that notion take root, she could be leading herself towards heartache again, the same kind of heartache she'd opened herself up to with Lucas, ignoring all the red flags around him and seeing only what she wanted, *needed*, to see.

But I'm not that desperate young girl anymore, Serena reminded herself.

But if that was true, why was she hoping Caleb's feelings were growing as much as hers?

Her head suddenly aching with confusion, it occurred to Serena then that she should insist on going on the tour with Mathilde alone and send Caleb to mingle with Thierry. That way she'd be able to find some perspective amongst her jumbled thoughts and get herself back on the page she was meant to be on. The page she *needed* to stay for her own protection. And she was never going to find that composure, or rationale, fizzing with delight at his nearness and with his every touch frying her nerve endings. But as she looked back at Caleb with that intent, she found she couldn't say the words.

How was she meant to chase him away and enforce that much-needed distance when all she wanted was exactly what she had, his closeness?

Caleb couldn't remember ever being as proud as he was of Serena that evening. She shone like the treasure she was, drawing everyone to her and alternately charming them with anecdotes about her siblings and impressing them with her extensive appreciation and knowledge of art. He hadn't been worried at all, but he knew she had been nervous about fitting into his world. Her body had been twanging with nerves as they'd arrived but she had overcome them to show off her beautiful self—just as she had overcome so much else. There wasn't a day that passed when he wasn't in awe of her strength, of the grit she had displayed to survive the traumas she'd suffered and remain a steady port for her siblings in the face of adversity from her stepmother. But he loved that she was now regaining her life, and herself.

Stealing her away the first moment he could, he led her outside to the gardens, a manicured paradise of lantern-lit stony pathways and low succulents. As soon as they were alone, he pulled her against him, satisfying as much as he could the need to have her taste on his tongue.

'I've been desperate to do that for an hour, but there were too many other people around,' he breathed as he pulled back and read the happiness and confidence radiating from her eyes. 'I think you've been an even bigger success tonight than the hotel. I told you there was no reason to be nervous.'

'I just didn't want to let you down,' she confessed.

'That would never happen. I didn't know you knew so much about the art world though.'

She shrugged. 'Marcia may have kept me from studying it at university, but I kept up learning as much as I could.'

'You caught Roberto Paloma's attention, and that's not easy," Caleb said, making reference to one of the other guests at the party, a renowned art gallery owner whom Serena had recognised the moment she set eyes on him from across the room. 'I watched him as you were speaking in there and he was impressed,' Caleb shared, hoping that she would draw further confidence from having gained the attention of a man she respected.

'I cannot believe you know him. Or that I was in the same room as him. I've admired him for years, Caleb.'

He smiled at her excitement. 'I think you mentioned that earlier.' Along with how she'd dreamed of visiting his galleries across Europe and loved the variety of artists he worked with. 'His next big venture is opening a gallery in London.'

'He told me.' The enthusiasm in her face dimmed, and she became very interested in smoothing down the lapels of his jacket. 'He actually said that if I was interested in a new career, he would like to hire me.'

'Really? I told you he was impressed.' But he wondered why she didn't look happier, why, if anything, she looked uneasy. 'Are you interested?'

She hesitated, conflict written all over her face. 'I

mean…working in the art world has always been my dream, but I'd resigned myself to it not happening. And now that we have a baby on the way… I want to be there to raise them and I know you want that too…'

His brow drew together. Was he the reason she was hesitant? Did she think he would prevent her from taking a job she so clearly wanted? But then again, after all those years of her stepmother, how could she not…

'What I want,' he began, speaking around the lump that had formed in his throat, because he hated that she even considered it a possibility that he would hold her back, 'is for you to be happy and to have everything you desire. I meant it when I said I didn't want to control you. And you've missed out on too much already to not take advantage of this opportunity.'

Her eyes searched his. 'Do you really mean that?' she asked, looking so hopeful and yet so frightened to hope.

'I do.'

Caleb hadn't even got the words out before she threw her arms around him and held on so tightly that he could feel the exaggerated beats of her heart. He smiled at her happiness, thrilled to be the source of it…but when exactly had her happiness become quite so important to him? More important, it seemed, than all else.

CHAPTER ELEVEN

CONTENT.

That was what Serena felt when she woke the following morning. It had been so long since she'd felt anything close to it that it took a moment to identify, but she smiled as she did. Because she was happy—as happy as she could ever remember being. Over the years she had learned to draw fulfilment from what she was fortunate to have in her life, like her brother and sister, and her evenings painting, but she hadn't been happy. But now it seemed as if her life was falling into place. Kit and Alexis were happy and cared for, her pregnancy was on the verge of entering its second trimester where the risk of miscarriage lessened, Caleb was proving to be a wonderful partner and she had just been offered her dream job.

She'd wanted to tell Caleb about the offer as soon as Roberto had made it, but she'd been wary—what if he didn't like the idea, after all she knew it mattered to him that their child wasn't left in the care of others? But he had been so supportive and encouraging, and that had touched her heart in ways she couldn't even explain.

Stretching out to find his warm body, she was disappointed when she didn't, only then remembering that the beach club was having an inspection and so he was leaving earlier than usual. He emerged from the dressing room, straightening the cuffs on his jacket, and Serena threw back the bedcovers, rising to wish him luck, but Caleb had gone still, his eyes fixed on something on the bed.

'What is it? What's wrong?'

She turned to see what had frozen his expression and felt ice course through her own veins as her eyes took in the red stain on the sheets. *Blood.* Her heart lurched and slowly, terror twisting its way around her, she lowered her eyes to her legs, gasping at the streaks of blood there too.

Her heart listed in her chest.

It was happening again.

The wait to find out what was happening was interminable.

Fear rattled in Serena's chest with every breath that she drew, the worst-case scenario unspooling in her mind on a loop as the jagged memories that had finally been fading from her mind returned with furious vengeance. Was this another baby she was destined to never know, another loss to be etched on her heart?

The only thing stopping her from falling apart completely was the pressure of Caleb's hand around hers, the knowledge that she wasn't on her own and didn't have to navigate the nightmare alone, as she had last time.

He hadn't wasted a second to spring into action back at the villa, guiding her to the car and driving to the hospital as if hellhounds were on his heels. He hadn't left her side, hadn't once let go of her hand, even as all she could do was stare at the blank wall opposite, her mind trapped somewhere between the past and the present and too scared of what the imminent future could hold to want to get there. For a moment there she had been really, truly happy. Excited for all of her tomorrows…

But wasn't this why she was so wary of happiness? Because she knew it never lasted. That eventually it always came crashing down.

A tear rolled down her cheek, and before she could swipe it away, Caleb did, moving from his chair to sit on the edge of the bed, taking her face in his hands. 'Hey. We don't know that there is anything wrong. There is every chance that everything is fine…'

'Please don't say that.' She couldn't hear those words. Couldn't let that injection of hope into her mind or her heart, not when she knew how hope turned so easily to ashes. 'Please don't tell me that everything is going to be OK, when you can't possibly know that.'

'OK.' He nodded, his eyes serious. 'How about I just tell you that whatever is happening, we'll deal with it together.'

Would they though?

Even as she sank into the warm, cocooning embrace of his arms, comforted by his strong presence and grateful for it, she couldn't help but fret over how long she would have him if the worst was happening. They had only married because she was pregnant, so what would happen if there was no longer a baby? Would the fact that they had grown so close hold any power? She knew he cared for her. She'd felt it…but as much as he gave with his body, he'd offered no words or promises to back up the actions. He had been clear their marriage was not an emotional affair and was primarily to safeguard their child's future. So, if there was no longer a baby…

It was on the tip of her tongue to voice her fears when the door opened and the doctor entered. Caleb held her hand tightly in his as she was examined, holding her eyes with his own, promising that she wasn't alone. *But for how long?*

'You and your baby are perfectly fine, Madame Morgenthau,' the doctor announced after a series of tests.

'You're sure?' Caleb demanded of him urgently, leaving no doubt that he had been as fearful for the well-being of their baby as she had.

'Perfectly.'

'But how?' Serena questioned, stunned to hear those words, because she had convinced herself the news would not be good. 'How is that possible? I was bleeding.'

'Bleeding is actually very common during the early stages of pregnancy,' he explained patiently. 'One in every four or five women experience it, and the majority go on to have a healthy pregnancy. At this time, I'm seeing nothing to suggest that cannot be the case for you too.' The words prompted a flicker of joy in her heart. She was relieved, most of all, that the baby was OK, but also that her relationship with Caleb was not under imminent threat. 'You can see for yourself, if you like,' he offered, angling the sonogram screen that he had been studying intently moments ago so that it faced them. 'That right there is your baby.' He smiled, pointing to a small curled shape in the centre of the screen. 'And this pulsing is his or her heartbeat, which you can hear is steady and strong.'

'Oh, my goodness.' Serena launched herself into a sitting position to better see the image, mesmerised by the tiny shape and the sound of its beating heart. Relief and delight poured through her, the image of her baby—safe and there—scattering the remainder of her fear the way light banished shadows. 'There you are.' She touched her fingertips to the screen, the tears that now fell solely of delight. 'My precious little one.'

'That's incredible,' Caleb whispered. 'Our baby.'

'I never got this far last time,' Serena told him quietly. And it was all the more wonderful to share it with him, and smiling into his eyes, it hit her how deeply she had fallen in love with him.

She didn't know how she hadn't realised it sooner. She'd certainly been aware of her feelings for him deepening. Her favourite time of day was when he returned home, and her heart fizzed and stomach overflowed every time he looked her way and delivered that slow smile before drawing her close for a kiss. She loved how he always asked about Kit and Alexis when he knew she'd spoken with them, and she loved how he made her feel so safe and cared for that she didn't always feel as if she had to be superstrong.

Only weeks ago, the thought of falling for Caleb had filled her with dread, but now she felt *stronger* for loving him. For having opened up her heart and letting him into it. He'd healed her, in so many ways, given her back so much of her life, showing her that it was OK for her to need someone and to lean on them.

But would he be willing to give her what she most wanted? A life with him.

Because he had told her explicitly that he didn't want love in his life, and Serena had promised that neither did she, so how could she now tell him that she had fallen more in love with him than she had ever thought possible?

But how could she *not* tell him?

Serena had *agreed* to a half life at eighteen because she had been vulnerable and scared, and doing so had kept her with Kit and Alexis, so she didn't regret it. But she'd had to repress so much of herself, her desires and dreams. She didn't want to deny herself again, and with her fears conquered and her past behind her, now was the time for her to start living a beautiful, full life.

Settling for less was no longer an option

Satisfied that Serena was resting after the ordeal of the morning, Caleb left the darkened bedroom and shut himself in the quiet privacy of the study, leaning back against the door and exhaling the ragged breath that he'd been holding all morning.

Never in his life had he been as scared as he was in that hospital, seeing Serena so pale and frightened, and unsure if he would get to meet his child, and his relief had never been as profound as when he watched the life force of his child pulsing steadily on the small screen. All of that and more still thudded through his chest.

It wasn't a surprise to Caleb that he cared. Of course he did. How could he not? Living in such close proximity, it was impossible to not develop human feelings, and he had already recognised his arrogance in imagining that he could manage his emotions for Serena and the pregnancy in the same clinical way he handled all else in his life. Even the pretence of a family required some degree of attachment. But caring for them, *her*, was one thing. It was acceptable. Just.

But the feelings pounding through him were more than that. They were violent and chaotic, desperate and fearful—everything Caleb had never wanted to feel again. The emotion he had spent his whole life avoiding after the pain of his childhood. The agony and the yearning. He didn't like it. He didn't want it.

He was happy feeling nothing...happier than when he'd felt everything. As a boy, the loss of his mother and indifference of his father had set loose emotional forces that had tormented him, and he refused to go back to that place of despair, where his feelings had complete control over him and his ability to function—to eat, sleep, live. He wouldn't allow himself to turn into his father, to become the wreck that he had become, controlled and defined by his torment. His father was pulled back together now, but that recovery had taken the better part of Caleb's life. He wouldn't live like that. He'd found a way as a boy to shut down the feeling, to end the agony, and would do so again now.

Forcing himself to sit, Caleb quickly formulated a plan and contacted his assistant with instructions and awaited her confirmation, ignoring the pinches of guilt to his gut. It had to be this way.

He had been so focused on Serena not developing feelings for him that he'd failed to keep watch over himself.

He had sensed last night that something was amiss, when he'd prioritised her happiness to take the job…

He had been too liberal with his time and emotions around Serena, and if he carried on in the same vein, he'd be no type of father to his child. He would be no better than his own, trapped in the storm of his own body and of no use to anyone. And how could he support Serena like that? She needed him to be strong so that she could be scared, as had been the case today, and he couldn't be strong for her if he was roiling inside, agitated with emotion that couldn't be soothed or contained. Emotion that led to only one place—destruction.

And it wasn't as if he was reneging on anything, just setting things back to how they were always supposed to have been, with him and Serena living their own lives. Not that telling himself that made him feel any better.

But by the time Chef Pierre was serving their evening meal, the plans were in place and all that was left to do was tell Serena. She was already seated at the table when he emerged, and he was pleased to see the colour had returned to her face. He forced himself to push away the thought that she would lose it again once he'd said his piece.

'How are you feeling?'

'Good. Better than I did earlier. And hungry,' she added, as a plate was set before her. 'I'm sorry that you missed your meetings today. I know how important they were.'

'Don't worry about it. Meetings can be rescheduled. Our baby was more important.' She smiled at him as she dug into another forkful, but Caleb's appetite was gone because he knew the moment had arrived. 'Speaking of that, I've arranged for you to return to London tomorrow.' He ignored the shock that came over her face. 'I spoke to Dr Newman and explained the situation, and she has time to see you tomorrow afternoon.'

'Is that really necessary? The doctor here said there was no reason for alarm. And I feel fine.'

'Dr Newman is the best in her field. I'd be happier if you saw her and got her opinion. And she is your primary physician.'

'OK,' Serena assented. 'I'll go to London, spend the night, see Kit and Alexis and come back the next day.'

'You don't need to do that. Once you're back in London, you should stay, get settled into the house. I've been assured its ready for us.'

Serena turned her eyes on him like twin spotlights that Caleb had to steel himself against. 'Are you coming back too?' He heard the tremor of unease enter her voice and guilt tightened his stomach.

'No. I'm going to stay here a while longer, whilst the final developments and inspections are happening. I'll return to London then.'

Her eyes hadn't left his face. He could feel them burning through his skin. 'Then I'll come back too. It could look strange us being in separate places so soon, no?'

Caleb shook his head. 'I don't think so. Everyone at the wedding saw your siblings. They're enough of a reason for you to be back in London without me. And this was always the plan. You in London, me wherever I'm needed,' he reminded her, summoning the detachment that had always come so easily to him and mentally snipping the threads that had grown between them. One day, hopefully, she would see that this was for the best.

'Yes, but that was before…' She cut herself off from whatever she'd been on the verge of saying, hurt creeping into her expression as she absorbed the detachment in his. She set down her fork and looked at him, almost pleadingly. 'I don't understand what's going on right now. Why don't you want me here? Why are you sending me away? Is it because of what happened earlier…'

'I told you. It's so you can see Dr Newman…'

'If your concern for me and the baby was all this was about, then you would be coming with me,' she asserted with conviction. 'What's really going on, Caleb? Tell me.'

'Nothing is going on…' But still he got up and walked away, unable to stand her expression any more, the way it tugged at him. He wished he could close his ears to the bewilderment in her voice as easily as he could avert his gaze.

'I don't believe you.' She followed him, searching his face with her anguished eyes. 'You're doing this for a reason. You're pushing me away. You're scared of something. I can see it. You're scared of what you felt today. *How much* you felt. Tell me I'm wrong.'

He wished he could.

'This marriage isn't about feelings, Serena. You know that,' he gritted out, keeping a tight hold on his emotions because she needed to see, as well as hear, that he didn't feel anything. And maybe with enough time, that would be true again.

'I know it wasn't meant to be. But that isn't something that either of us can control.' She pulled in a breath, reaching for him and the blaze of her fingertips against him...

Caleb resisted and savoured in the same moment. He knew he would never touch her again.

'Today, at the hospital, Caleb, I was so scared. I was scared about the baby, of course, but I was also scared about what would happen between us if I did lose the baby. Because as much as I know we got married to protect our child and keep me in my brother and sister's lives, the truth is I would want to be married to you even if those reasons didn't exist.' Her eyes filled with fear and with hope. 'Because I love you.'

For a second the words seemed to warm him, before the expected coldness struck, as if his chest had been packed with ice. 'You promised that wouldn't happen.'

She nodded. 'I believed that when I said it. I thought I'd endured too much loss and couldn't stand the risk of anymore. The last thing I wanted was to put my heart in harm's way again. But being with you, opening up to you...it's changed that. Taken me back to who I was before it all got so hard, and as frightening as it still is to know that I could lose again, it's not scary enough to stop me from wanting to try. Not anymore. Not with you.' All the feeling he was trying so hard to suppress threatened. 'I spent so long living a life that wasn't what I wanted, Caleb. I don't want to do that again. You're the one who told me that I didn't have to, that I could have everything I wanted, and this is what I want. Happiness. Family. Passion. Love. With you.'

Love. She was asking for the one thing she knew he couldn't give. Didn't want to give. He cared for her, more deeply than he'd cared for anyone, and he'd happily give her all else that he could, but love? The word alone was enough to make him lock down. What had loving ever brought anyone in his life? Desolation and despair. He wouldn't ever invite that in.

'I can't give you what you want, Serena. I'm sorry.'

'Can't?' she demanded. 'Or won't? I know you're scared, Caleb. It's frightening for me too. But won't you even try? I know what we have matters to you. I *know* it. Isn't that worth trying?'

'I have been honest with you from the beginning, Serena,' he stated, holding on to his emotion by a thread whilst keeping her at bay with his cool tone. 'I never lied about what this could be, or what I was willing to offer. Not once.'

'That's it? That's all you have to say? She looked so despairing, and so disappointed in him. *See,* he wanted to say, *this is what love does. What love is.* She stepped back, looking as though she'd taken a punch to the stomach. As wrecked, if not more, than she had looked earlier, and it tore at him to be the cause of it. But that was what happened when you let love in. It was why he never would. She turned away so he couldn't see the tears that shook her shoulders, but when she turned back, it was anger, not pain, boiling in her eyes, and he loathed himself for forcing her back to her guarded stance, to that place where she refused to let anyone see her flounder. 'I guess I will go back to London then. But tonight. And not as your wife.'

In a single, deliberate movement she removed the

rings from her finger and put them on the table, and the act landed like a grenade in his gut.

His heart banged so powerfully; he was sure it bruised his insides. 'Serena…'

'No.' She held up a silencing hand. 'We've said everything that needs to be said. This is where we are. You're not willing to offer me more and I refuse to settle for less. So, this is the only way forwards. Goodbye Caleb.'

Half an hour later, he watched silently as she walked out of the door, and though his despair grew with every step away from him that she took, he let her go because he had to, because he was too afraid to do anything other than that.

CHAPTER TWELVE

CALEB'S EYES WERE gritty with tiredness as he glanced at the clock and saw that it was nearly midnight. *That explains that.* He'd been working for almost eighteen hours, and on barely any sleep. But instead of reaching for his jacket and returning to the villa, and his bed, he began scrolling through his emails, filling his mind with more work.

Just like your father.

The comparison landed like a blow, the uncomfortable truth forcing him back in his chair. He was doing exactly as his father had, wasn't he? Burying himself in business in an attempt to forget about his feelings, pretend they didn't exist.

Only they did exist.

And he was tired of pretending not to feel them. To not feel the ache and agony.

He'd thought he would feel better, more like himself, once he had wrested back control of the situation and his emotions—and he had. At first. But very quickly that sense of victory at mastering his feelings, his heart, had fled, and far from feeling on safe ground, he felt more lost than ever before.

Lost and lonely and empty.

Because he hadn't just pushed Serena away emotionally, he had pushed her all the way out of his life. So much of him had revolted at letting her walk out the door unchallenged, but forcing her to stay hadn't been an option, regardless of what she'd promised, or what agreement she had signed her name to. It was bad enough that he'd cornered her into the marriage in the first place; he couldn't force her to remain in a situation that didn't provide the emotional sustenance that she needed. Deserved. It would be nice to think that if he'd known then what he knew about her life now, he would never have strong-armed her into the stupid arrangement, only he couldn't say for sure. But he was a better man now, and after everything she'd been through, Serena had earned the right to have the life she wanted. And since the only way for her to find that happiness was for him to let her and their baby go, that was what he'd done.

But he throbbed with how badly he missed her. She was still the first thing he thought of each day, and each evening he searched the villa for any trace of her; her scent, a missed belonging.

Did I make a terrible mistake?

Caleb prowled to the window, staring into the darkness. He had always maintained that it was preferable to feel nothing, to keep his heart safe and separate, but forcing himself to be honest, Caleb had never felt more content or settled in his life, more at peace than during these past weeks with Serena.

He'd been scared from the beginning of how much she had made him feel, thinking it was a bad thing, that it would lead him back to a place he wanted to avoid at all costs, but it was only when he had feared that he was losing her, and the baby, that the chaos had returned. It was only now, without her, that he couldn't eat or sleep. Function.

It was letting her in, *loving her*, that had brought him peace. Just as it was finding a new love with Ellie that had healed his father. Helped him find peace after so many years of hurt. Caleb just hadn't realised that until now.

He drew in a sharp breath at the realisation, but didn't hide from it or try to fight it off. Because it was true. He loved Serena. He suspected he had for a while.

For as long as he could remember, love was something to be avoided, something that would only invite chaos into his body and soul, but it was the opposite that was true.

Serena said that he had given her life back to her, but she'd brought him back to life too, he realised with a jolt of his heart. It was because of her that he'd started to heal, to forgive himself for his past mistakes with Charlotte and see himself in a different way. The only reason that he believed he could be a good father to their child was because of her, because of her faith and trust in him, the love she had given so freely and fearlessly.

But when she'd been brave enough to ask for what she needed and wanted, he'd been a coward. He'd denied her, pushed her away, let her believe that she wasn't loved, and that made him sick to his stomach, because if there was one person on the planet who deserved to be loved, it was Serena.

He needed to fix it. Whatever it took, he would fix it. Because he'd been wrong. So wrong. And he didn't want to waste a minute to make it right again.

She had done the right thing.

That was what Serena kept telling herself. What she had to keep reminding herself. Each morning when she woke and another day without Caleb stretched endlessly ahead. Each time she looked at the sonogram shot of their baby and thought of all the moments she wouldn't get to share with him. Each night as she lay in bed alone and aching, missing his warm presence beside her.

She hated being all alone again…

But leaving had been the only thing to do.

She had held out her heart for him to accept, and he hadn't wanted it. Which was the outcome Serena had feared, and yet some part of her had still hoped that the closeness they'd built would be enough to change his mind about not wanting love in his life. Because she really thought their relationship had changed him. Serena knew he had felt as much terror and joy as she had in the hospital. She knew it wasn't only her heart that had become invested in the relationship… Caleb just wasn't willing to accept that.

He didn't want it to be the truth. He didn't want to love her.

And Serena couldn't force him to.

She could have stayed and waited to see if, with a little more time, Caleb did change his mind, but that would only have been short-changing herself, and she'd already lost so much time that to spend another minute of her life not living it the way she wanted, without the love that she was now brave enough to admit that she craved, was impossible. Especially now that she remembered how exhilarating it was to love. How fulfilling.

Even though it had ended in the way she'd most wanted to avoid, with her heart tearing apart, she wouldn't be flattened by that pain. The scar on her heart was a mark of bravery, of how she'd risked herself for love, and despite the pain being worse than anything she had endured before—deeper and sharper, persisting through all hours of the day and night—Serena knew she could survive it. Would survive it. The time she'd spent with Caleb had shown her that. She was a fighter, a survivor, and she would never forget that again. Never doubt her own power again.

She would make it through this, without closing herself off to the future. She would build a good life for herself and her child, chase happiness because she deserved it and without the fear of losing it, even if there remained a part of her that was always sad that she hadn't been able to find that happiness with Caleb…

That was why, after days of lying curled up on Evie's sofa, she'd taken the step of going to the new house, because she had to move on and move forwards. It was a beautiful Georgian house in Holland Park, only a short walk from where Kit and Alexis lived with her stepmother. She had just finished unpacking and exploring the space that was now her home, when there was a knock at the door.

'Caleb…' It was the strangest moment of déjà vu, to find him looming on her doorstep once again, and despite the elation filling in her heart, she quickly tensed, not interested in letting history repeat itself. 'If you're here to twist my arm into coming back and keeping up the pretence...'

'I'm not,' he said, holding up a hand as though swearing to that, and it was then she noticed the crescent shadows beneath his eyes, his stubble an inch thicker than normal, and his paleness beneath his tan. But his eyes glowed with his characteristic determination. 'All I'm asking for is five minutes of your time because there are some things I need to say.'

She knew he could accomplish a lot in five minutes, and yet it was such a small thing to ask for that refusing seemed petty. And she couldn't avoid him forever—not when they had a child to raise. 'Alright.'

But Serena was wary as she stepped back to let him inside, and as he followed her into the living room, she chose to stand as far from his magnetic force field as possible, trying to keep her heart from rioting out of control.

'I'm sorry,' he said, startling her because they were the last words she had expected to hear. 'I'm so sorry, Serena. For pushing you away and for saying nothing when you told me you loved me. I shouldn't have let a single second go by without telling you the same, but instead I pushed you away even more, because I was scared. Scared of how much I loved hearing you tell me that and scared of how much I felt for you.' He came a step closer, and she knew she should maintain a safe distance between them, but was too stunned to move. 'Serena, for as long as I can remember, I've thought of love as something destructive, something that causes chaos and weakness and would weaken me if I let it. I watched what loving my mother did to my father after she left, and even though I didn't remember her, I know what it did to me. There was this gaping hole that nothing could heal, and it made me yearn for something so badly that I thought I'd die from the force of it. I *never* wanted to feel that again. That desperation and chaos inside me, so I pulled back from everyone, from wanting anything from them. But then came you, and I don't really know what happened. Just that it happened easily, but when you asked me to name it, all I could think of was all that bad from my childhood. But I do love you, Serena. I love your heart and strength and how hard you fight. I love how much you love Kit and Alexis, and how much I know you will love and protect our child. And, if there was no baby, I would still love you. I would still want you at my side.'

Serena didn't know when she'd started crying; only realised her face was wet as her pain and longing fought through her control. Hearing him explain the effects of his childhood was heartbreaking. It wasn't hard to understand that boy—rejected and scared to love and ask for more, to accept more, in case it made him vulnerable again—still lived inside of him. No wonder he'd been frightened of the love building between them, and been so unwilling to acknowledge it. 'I know what I did was awful, but I wanted you to know the truth. To know that you are loved. And to tell you that if you could find it within you to forgive and let me back into your life, I would never make you doubt it again. I would never let you down again.'

The words were perfect, everything she'd wanted him

to say to her all those days ago. But he hadn't, and that silence had wounded her more than words could express, and as badly as she wanted to sink into him now, could she trust him?

'You let me walk out of the door, Caleb. Out of your life and our marriage.' Guilty colour slashed across his cheeks and his head bowed with the weight of his regret, but the weight of her pain was heavy too. 'You didn't even try to stop me.'

'I wanted to. At least a part of me did. But I was too scared.' His eyes pleaded with her. 'I wasn't ready to accept how I felt. I regret it, Serena. More than anything I've ever done before. I'll regret it forever. But I want to fix it. That's why I'm here. To make it better. You deserve to have exactly the life you want, Serena. A life full of love and passion and happiness, and I want to give you that life.'

'And what happens the next time you feel scared?' she demanded, trembling with the force of her feeling. Her hope and her fear. 'When you get overwhelmed by all your emotions? Are you going to push me away again?'

'Never. Never again.'

'Because it's not just me, Caleb. It's Kit and Alexis too. They have lost just as much as me, and in another few months there will be another little person, and I won't do that to them. I won't put them through it.'

'It won't happen, Serena.' He stepped closer again, his eyes blazing. 'I promise. I am here. I am in this. Every day, I will be here. With you. For you. In love with you. Trust me. *Please trust me.* I know I haven't done much to deserve it, but trust me. I won't let you down. I love you. And I won't ever let you go ever again.'

'Say that again.'

He took a breath. 'I will never let you go…'

'No. Not that part.' Serena offered him a little smile. 'The part about loving me.'

Taking her face in his hands, Caleb looked deep into her eyes with his own honest gaze, where she saw nothing but the truth. Pain. But also love. 'I love you, Serena. I love everything about you, with everything that I am. You, and this little one, were the last thing I thought I wanted, but you're the best things that have ever happened to me.'

It was impossible to last a moment more without throwing her arms around him and sinking into the heat and safety of his body. 'I missed you, Caleb.'

'Nowhere near as much as I've missed you,' he breathed, pressing kisses to her mouth, her cheeks, her eyelids. 'My life was empty without you, Serena. I never want to go back to that.'

'You'll never have to,' she promised, holding tight and smiling. Because whilst she had no idea what life would throw at them, Serena trusted—no, she *knew*—it would be alright because she had him.

Because they had each other.

EPILOGUE

WHO KNEW THAT a toddler's birthday party would create such widespread detritus?

As they did their usual divide-and-conquer routine, and Caleb put their three-year-old daughter to bed, Serena tackled the mess downstairs, clearing the rooms, tidying the new stack of toys, stacking the dishwasher and wiping down the counters. By the time she heard her husband descending the stairs, their living space was gleaming again.

'Did Frankie go down okay?'

He smiled indulgently, sliding his arms around her from behind. 'She was fast asleep in my arms before her head went anywhere near her pillow. She was worn-out.'

'She did have a big day.'

'I cannot believe how much she relished being the centre of attention at her party. I know she *always* loves being the centre of attention,' he added quickly, 'but she revelled in it even more than usual today.'

Serena smiled, resting her head against his shoulder. 'When we decided to name her after my mum, I hoped she would have a little of her spirit, but we definitely got more than we bargained for. I wouldn't change her though, not a single thing.' Even if she was *exhausting*!

'Me neither,' he agreed, pressing a warm kiss to her cheek. 'She's perfect, just like her very beautiful, very sexy mother.' Serena spun in his arms, feeling his arousal, and without delay heat swept through her body, delighted by the thought of surrendering to him. 'Please tell me everyone has left,' he breathed, seizing her mouth for a burning kiss.

'Mm-hmm. Kit is staying at his friends down the road. Your father and Ellie have gone back to the hotel, and Evie is dropping Alexis off at Marcia's.'

Marcia had been invited to the party, but preexisting plans meant she hadn't been able to attend. She had sent a gift though, a gesture that Serena appreciated. The years hadn't brought them any closer—too much had passed between them for there to be closeness—but they had learned to respect one another and had built a civil relationship for the sake of Kit and Alexis. It was peaceful, which was enough.

'Excellent. I think we should make the most of this rare moment of peace and quiet—no toddler running around, no teenagers wandering in and out—and start practicing to make another perfect human all over again.'

Serena arched her eyebrows, smiling. 'That's really what you want? Another baby?'

'Yes.' He nodded, barely able to hide his eagerness.

He'd been talking about extending their family for a while. He loved being a father to Frankie and a surrogate father-cum-big brother to Kit and Alexis. And Serena loved watching him do it. He was so sure and steady, never holding back in his affection or guidance. Watching him, it was hard to believe he'd ever been worried about being a good father.

Becoming a dad had also helped his relationship with his own father. It was in the high emotion surrounding Frankie's birth that Caleb had finally found the courage to broach the matter of his childhood with his father. As Caleb suspected, his father had no recollection of blaming him and had been horrified to hear about his actions. His apology had been swift and sincere, and his explanation of his heartache had been met with understanding from Caleb. His father had spent every day since working hard to heal the rift between them and to be the best father and grandfather possible, and it hadn't taken long for them to overcome all the guilt and pain they both carried from that long-ago time in their lives.

'I'm glad you feel that way because I found out today that I'm six weeks pregnant.'

She watched his reaction; his eyes widening with disbelief and then glowing with delight 'You are?' Emotion shimmered in his gaze as he looked quickly down at her stomach. 'Wait. Six weeks?'

Serena had to laugh. 'I know. It's crazy.' Six weeks ago, they had been on the way back from their biannual trip to Australia and had stopped in Singapore for a few days. 'There's just something about you, me and Singapore that seems to be a very potent combination.' She laughed, smoothing her hand over his short hair.

'I love you so much, Serena,' he said earnestly, claiming her lips for one of the deep kisses she loved, because it seemed to say he couldn't get enough of her. 'And I love our family so much.'

She knew he did. There was never any doubt about that in her mind, not with all the ways he'd changed his life to make them his priority, but it was always so much fun when he demonstrated it too.

'Show me how much,' she breathed, leaning in to him to curl her arms around his neck and touch her lips to his, and it wasn't a request she had to make twice.

* * * * *

Did Pregnant and Conveniently Wed
have you enthralled?
Then don't miss Rosie Maxwell's other
dramatic stories!

An Heir for the Vengeful Billionaire
Billionaire's Runaway Wife

Available now!

Get up to 4 Free Books!

We'll send you 2 free books from each series you try PLUS a free Mystery Gift.

FREE
Value Over
$25

Both the **Harlequin Presents** and **Harlequin Medical Romance** series feature exciting stories of passion and drama.

YES! Please send me 2 FREE novels from Harlequin Presents or Harlequin Medical Romance and my FREE gift (gift is worth about $10 retail). After receiving them, if I don't wish to receive any more books, I can return the shipping statement marked "cancel." If I don't cancel, I will receive 6 brand-new larger-print novels every month and be billed just $7.19 each in the U.S., or $7.99 each in Canada, or 4 brand-new Harlequin Medical Romance Larger-Print books every month and be billed just $7.19 each in the U.S. or $7.99 each in Canada, a savings of 20% off the cover price. It's quite a bargain! Shipping and handling is just 50¢ per book in the U.S. and $1.25 per book in Canada.* I understand that accepting the 2 free books and gift places me under no obligation to buy anything. I can always return a shipment and cancel at any time. The free books and gift are mine to keep no matter what I decide.

Choose one: ☐ **Harlequin Presents Larger-Print**
(176/376 BPA G36Y)

☐ **Harlequin Medical Romance**
(171/371 BPA G36Y)

☐ **Or Try Both!**
(176/376 & 171/371 BPA G36Z)

Name (please print)

Address   Apt. #

City   State/Province   Zip/Postal Code

Email: Please check this box ☐ if you would like to receive newsletters and promotional emails from Harlequin Enterprises ULC and its affiliates. You can unsubscribe anytime.

Mail to the **Harlequin Reader Service:**
IN U.S.A.: P.O. Box 1341, Buffalo, NY 14240-8531
IN CANADA: P.O. Box 603, Fort Erie, Ontario L2A 5X3

Want to explore our other series or interested in ebooks? Visit www.ReaderService.com or call 1-800-873-8635.

HPHM25